訓練聽力　增加字彙

英語聽力是學習英語的重要一環，必須提早開始，長期訓練。而且要有計劃地反覆練習，絕不能只學聽單自認圖片，一定要聽句子，而且要逐漸拉長句子的內容，才能學習到英語的真諦。

本書分為〔上〕、〔中〕、〔下〕引導學生在學習上循序漸進，逐步加強，期望能在12年國教國中會考考試中，一舉拿下聽力的滿分。本書的另一特色為在快樂學習中增加單字的記憶和使用能力，透過反覆的聽力測驗，不但大量增加字彙的累積，在不知不覺中也學會了說與寫的能力，可謂一舉數得，而且輕鬆易得。

為減輕學生的聽力障礙，本書將考題敘述的每個句子及答案，都精心譯為中文，以供學生參考。

1. 隨時注意 7 個 W：who, when, what, where, which, why, how

也就是人、時、事、地、物、原因、狀態

2. 能夠與不能 (ability and inability)

常用字詞有：can, be able to, could, can't, couldn't, not be able to, neither

1) A: How many languages can you speak?

B: I can/am able to speak three languages fluently.

翻譯：A：你能說幾種語言？

B：我能流利的說三種語言。

2) A: Has he bought a new house?

B: No. He's never been able to save money.

翻譯：A：他買新房子了嗎？

B：不，他永遠沒有能力存錢。

3) A: I couldn't do the homework. It was too difficult.

B: Neither could I.

翻譯：A：我不會做作業。太難了。

B：我也不會。

3. 勸告與建議 (advice and suggestion)

常用字詞有：had better, I think, let's, OK, yes, good idea, sure, why not,

1) A: I've got a headache today.

B: You'd better go to see the doctor./I think you should go to see the doctor.

翻譯：A：我今天頭痛。

B：你最好去看醫生。我想你應該去看醫生。

2) A: I've got a terrible stomachache.

B: You'd better not go on working.

A: OK./All right./Thank you for your advice.

翻譯：A：我的胃痛死了。

B：你最好不要上班。

C：好的/沒問題/謝謝你的勸告。

3) A: Let's go, shall we?

B: Yes, let's./I'm afraid it's too early.

翻譯：A：我們走吧，要不要？

B：好，走吧。/我怕太晚了。

4) A: What/How about going fishing now?

B: That's a good idea./That sounds interesting./Sure. Why not?

翻譯：A：現在去釣魚怎麼樣？

B：好主意。/聽起來很有趣。/當然，有何不可？

5) A: Let's go to the concert.

B: I don't feel like it. Why don't we go to the beach instead?

翻譯：A：我們去聽音樂會吧。

B：我不想去。我們為什麼不去海邊？

4. 同意與不同意 (agreement and disagreement)

常用字詞有：I think so. I hope so. I don't think so. I agree. I don't agree. So can I. Me too. Neither can I. I can't, either.

1) A: The book is interesting.

B: I think so, too.

翻譯：A：這本書很有趣。

B：我也這麼想。

2) A: Do you think people will be able to live on the moon in the future?

B: I hope so, but I don't think so.

翻譯：A：你認為人類將來能住到月球上嗎？

B：希望如此，但我不認為能夠。

3) A: This lesson is interesting, isn't it?

B: I don't think so./I'm afraid I can't agree with you./I'm afraid I don't quite agree with you./I'm afraid it isn't.

翻譯：A：這堂課很有趣，不是嗎？

B：我不這樣認為。恐怕我無法同意你。我恐怕不十分同意你。恐怕不是這樣。

4) A: I can swim well.

B: So can I./Me too.

翻譯：A：我很會游泳。

B：我也是。

5) A: I can't play the guitar.

B: Neither can I./I can't, either.

翻譯：A：我不會彈吉他。

B：我也不會。

5. 道歉 (Apology)

常用字詞有：Sorry. I'm sorry about ....

A: Sorry./I'm terribly sorry about that.

B: That's all right./Never mind./Don't worry.

翻譯：A：抱歉。關於那件事我非常抱歉。

B：沒關係。不要放在心上。不要擔心。

6. 讚賞 (Appreciation)

常用字詞有：That's a good idea. That sounds interesting. Fantastic! Amazing! Well done！That's wonderful.

1) A: I've got the first prize.

B: Well done！/You deserved to win./That's wonderful news.

翻譯：A：我得第一名。

B：真棒。你實至名歸。真是個棒消息。

2) A: We had a surprise birthday party on Saturday afternoon.

B: That was a super afternoon.

翻譯：A：星期六下午的生日聚會令人驚喜。

B：那是個超棒的下午。

3) A: He broke the world record for the two mile run.

B: Fantastic!/Amazing!

翻譯：A：他在兩英哩賽跑打破世界紀錄。

B：了不起。又驚又喜。

7. 肯定與不肯定 (certainty and uncertainty)

常用字詞有：sure, not sure, perhaps, maybe, possible, possibly,

1) A: Are you sure?

B: Yes, I am./No, I'm not.

翻譯：A：你確定嗎？

B：是的，我確定。不，我不確定。

2) A: When will Mary go to school?

B: Perhaps/Maybe she'll go at eight.

翻譯：A：Mary 何時上學？

B：或許 8 歲。

3) A: His ambition is to be an architect.

B: He'll possibly go to university after he leaves school.

翻譯：A：他的願望是當建築師。

B：他離開學校後可能要念大學。

8. 比較 (Comparison)

常用字詞有：as...as..., not so... as..., more... than..., less...than...,

1) A: How tall is Sue?

B: 1.6 meters. She's not so tall as Jane.

A: What about Mary?

B: She's as tall as Sue.

翻譯：A：Sue 身高多少。

B：160 公分。她不像 Jane 那麼高。

A：那 Mary 呢？

B：她跟 Sue 一樣高。

2) A: Which is more important, electricity or water?
B: It's hard to say.
翻譯：A：哪個比較重要，水還是電？
B：很難說。

9. 關心 (Concern)

常用字詞有：Is anything wrong? What's the matter? What's wrong with ....? What's the matter with ....? How's ......?

1) A: What's wrong with you?/What's the matter with you?
B: I've got a cold.
翻譯：A：你怎麼了？
B：我感冒了。

2) A: How's your mother?
B: She's worse than yesterday.
A: I'm sorry to hear that. Don't worry too much. She'll get better soon.
翻譯：A：令堂狀況如何。
B：她比昨天更糟了。
A：我聽了很遺憾。不用太擔心。她很快就會好一些。

4) A: What's the matter?
B: I can't find my car key.
翻譯：A：發生甚麼事？
B：我找不到汽車鑰匙。

10. 詢問 (Inquiries)

常用字詞有：How, when, where, who, why, what

1) A: Excuse me, how can I get to the railway station?
B: Take a No. 41 bus.
翻譯：A：對不起，要如何到火車站去？
B：搭 41 號公車。

2) A: Excuse me. When does the next train leave for Kaohsuing?
B: 10 a.m.

翻譯：A：對不起。去高雄的下一班火車是甚麼時候？
B：上午十點。

3) A: What's the weather like today?
B: It'll rain this afternoon.
翻譯：A：今天天氣如何？
B：下午會下雨。

4) A: How far is your home from the school?
B: Five minutes by bike.
翻譯：A：你家距離學校有多遠？
B：騎單車5分鐘。

11. 意向 (Intentions)

常用字詞有：I'd like ..., Would you like to...? What do you want ...?

1) A: What do you want to be in the future?
B: I want to be a businessman.
翻譯：A：你將來想當甚麼？
B：我想當生意人。

2) A: Would you like to work at the South Pole in the future?
B: Yes, we'd love to.
翻譯：A：你將來喜歡在南極工作嗎？
B：是的，我會喜歡。

3) A: I'd like fried eggs with peas and pork, too.
B: OK.
翻譯：A：我想要豆子、豬肉炒蛋。
B：沒問題。

12. 喜歡、不喜歡/偏愛 (Likes, dislikes and preferences)

常用字詞有：like, dislike, prefer, enjoy

1) A: Which kind of apples do you prefer, red ones or green ones?
B: Green ones.
翻譯：A：你比較喜歡哪一種蘋果，紅的還是綠的?
B：綠的。

2) A: Do you enjoy music or dance?
B: I enjoy music.
翻譯：A：你喜歡音樂還是跳舞？
B：我喜歡音樂。

3) A: How did you like the play?
B: It was wonderful.
翻譯：A：這齣戲你覺得如何？
B：很棒。

13. 提供 (Offers)

常用字詞有：Can I ....? Let me .... What can I ...? Would you like ...?

1) A: Can I help you?
B: Yes, please.
翻譯：A：可以幫你忙嗎？
B：是的，謝謝。

2) A: Let me help you.
B: Thanks.
翻譯：A：我來幫你忙。
B：謝謝。

3) A: Would you like a drink?
B: That's very kind of you.
翻譯：A：要來杯飲料嗎？
B：你真好意。

4) A: Shall I get a trolley for you?
B: No, thanks.
翻譯：A：要我拿輛手推車給你嗎？
B：不用，謝謝。

全新國中會考英語聽力精選 上冊
目　　錄

測驗題

全文翻譯

全新國中會考英語聽力精選(上)

Unit 1

I 、Listen and choose the right picture.（根據你所聽到的內容,選出相應的圖片。）（6 分）

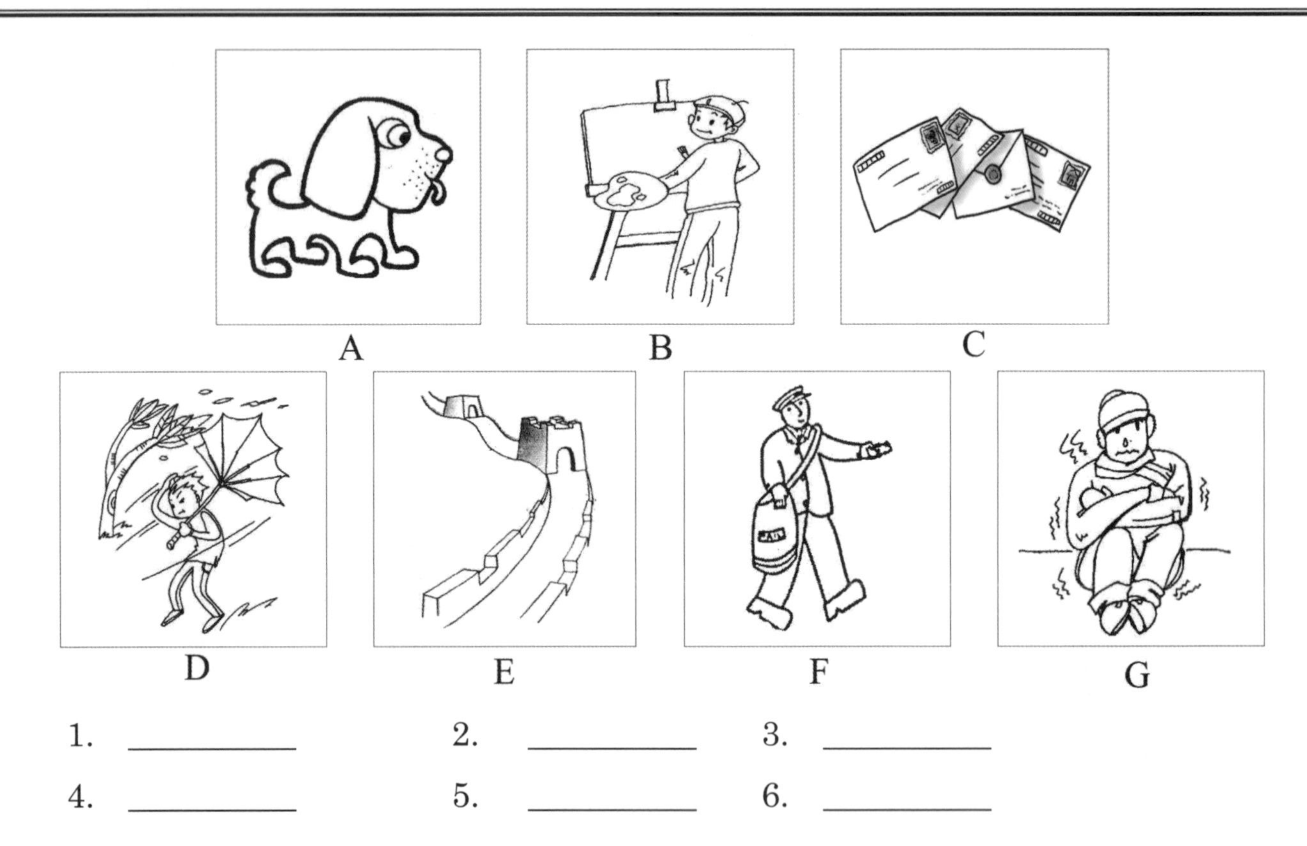

1. ________　2. ________　3. ________

4. ________　5. ________　6. ________

II 、Listen and choose the best response to the sentence you hear.（根據你所聽到的句子,選出最恰當的應答句。）（6 分）

(　) 7. (A)So do I.　(B)So could I.
(C)Neither do I.　(D)Neither could I.

(　) 8. (A)About 10 minutes.　(B)In 10 minutes.
(C)10-minute walk.　(D)For 10 minutes.

(　) 9. (A)You'd better watch more TV.
(B)You'd better sleep late.
(C)You'd better sleep earlier.
(D)You'd better not go to see the doctor.

(　) 10. (A)That's a good idea. (B)That's right.
(C)That's all right. (D)Of course not.

(　) 11. (A)I hope so. (B)I hope not.
(C)I agree with you. (D)I don't like.

(　) 12. (A)At two o'clock. (B)For one hour.
(C)In two hours later. (D)Two hours.

Ⅲ、Listen to the dialogue and choose the best answer to the question you hear.（根據你所聽到的對話和問題,選出最恰當的答案。）(6分)

(　) 13. (A)In the bookstore. (B)In the reading room.
(C)In the physics lab. (D)In the computer room.

(　) 14. (A)Because of the weather. (B)Because of his hobby.
(C)Because of his job. (D)Because of his age.

(　) 15. (A)In the classroom. (B)In the library.
(C)In the hospital. (D)In the dining room.

(　) 16. (A)Mary. (B)Peter.
(C)Tom. (D)John.

(　) 17. (A)At ten o'clock. (B)Before ten o'clock.
(C)Before twelve o'clock. (D)At about twelve o'clock.

(　) 18. (A)A secretary. (B)A waitress.
(C)A librarian. (D)A shop assistant.

Ⅳ、Listen to the dialogue and decide whether the following statements are True (T) or False (F).（判斷下列句子內容是否符合你所聽到的對話內容,符合的用"T"表示,不符合的用"F"表示。）(6分)

(　) 19. London is the largest city in the world.

(　) 20. London is very large, so it is difficult to see something interesting in the city centre.

(　) 21. Mandy liked the London buses because they went very fast.

(　) 22. Mandy saw David Beckham in the museum.

(　) 23. It was raining when Mandy was on the River Thames.

( ) 24. Mandy has brought some photos that she took in China Town with her.

V、Listen and fill in the blanks.(根據你所聽到的內容,用適當的單詞完成下面的句子。每空格限填一詞。)(6分)

25. Mary was often ill so she wanted to be ___________. But she didn't know what to do.

26. Miss Black told Mary that she must look after herself and then do something ___________ for her health.

27. Mary should do morning ___________ and play sports.

28. Mary must eat fruit and ___________ and wash hands before meals.

29. Mary shouldn't go to school without ___________ in the morning.

30. Mary shouldn't watch TV too ___________, read in the sun or stay up late and so on.

全新國中會考英語聽力精選(上)

Unit 2

I、Listen and choose the right picture.(根據你所聽到的內容，選出相應的圖片。)(6分)

1. ________ 2. ________ 3. ________
4. ________ 5. ________ 6. ________

II、Listen and choose the best response to the sentence you hear.(根據你所聽到的句子，選出最恰當的應答句。)(6分)【第10題，你所聽到的SPCA是指防止動物虐待協會】

( ) 7. (A)We should do that softly and gently with our two arms.
(B)Give them some puppy biscuits to chew every day.
(C)Don't hold them in your arms. Stop!
(D)I'm sorry to hear that.

( ) 8. (A)There are so many puppies here. (B)The black and white one.
(C)Take them away, please. (D)Are you sure about them?

(　) 9. (A)They help them catch thieves.
(B)They help them cross the streets.
(C)They help them hunt animals for food.
(D)They help them guide the caves.

(　) 10. (A)They take dogs to people's homes.
(B)They take bad people to police stations.
(C)They find homeless animals and look after them.
(D)They promise to make sick animals better.

(　) 11. (A)They give their pets a lot of water to drink.
(B)They give their pets some bones to chew.
(C)They hold their pets gently and look after them well.
(D)They leave their pets in the streets and never take them back.

(　) 12. (A)Yes, they did. (B)No, they didn't.
(C)Yes, they do. (D)No, they don't.

Ⅲ、Listen to the dialogue and choose the best answer to the question you hear.
（根據你所聽到的對話和問題，選出最恰當的答案。）(6 分)

(　) 13. (A)A red shirt with long sleeves. (B)A white shirt with short sleeves.
(C)A blue shirt with short sleeves. (D)A white shirt with long sleeves.

(　) 14. (A)A businessman. (B)An astronaut.
(C)A pilot. (D)A sportsman.

(　) 15. (A)On the bus. (B)In the car.
(C)At the crossing . (D)On the street.

(　) 16. (A)Paint the walls. (B)Make tables.
(C)Make the roof. (D)Decorate the walls.

(　) 17. (A)By ferry. (B)By train.
(C)By underground. (D)Through Sightseeing Tunnel.

(　) 18. (A)Spring. (B)Summer.
(C)Autumn. (D)Winter.

Ⅳ、Listen to the passage and decide whether the following statements are True (T) or False (F).（判斷下列句子內容是否符合你所聽到的短文內容，符合的用"T"表示，不符合的用"F"表示。）(6 分)

(　) 19. Both people and animals have homes.

(　) 20. The woodchuck lives in two rooms.

(　) 21. All animals live on the ground.

(　) 22. Birds usually live in nests in trees.

(　) 23. Bees don't work hard to build their house.

(　) 24. The zoo is no home for animals.

Ⅴ、Listen and complete the poem.（根據你所聽到的內容，用適當的單詞完成下面的詩歌。每空格限填一詞。）(6 分)

My two little pets

My two little pets
Are small and __25__
They like to jump
Up and down.

Round and round
They go on their wheel
And their __26__ treat
Is apple peel.
As I sit
And watch one play
The other __27__
A bed of hay.

Light and soft

They like __28__ hay
To keep them warm
From night till day.

My friends tell me
They look __29__ squirrels.
But I still __30__
Like my two fluffy chipmunks.

25. __________ 26. __________ 27. __________

28. __________ 29. __________ 30. __________

全新國中會考英語聽力精選(上)

Unit 3

Ⅰ、Listen and choose the right picture.（根據你所聽到的內容，選出相應的圖片）（5分）

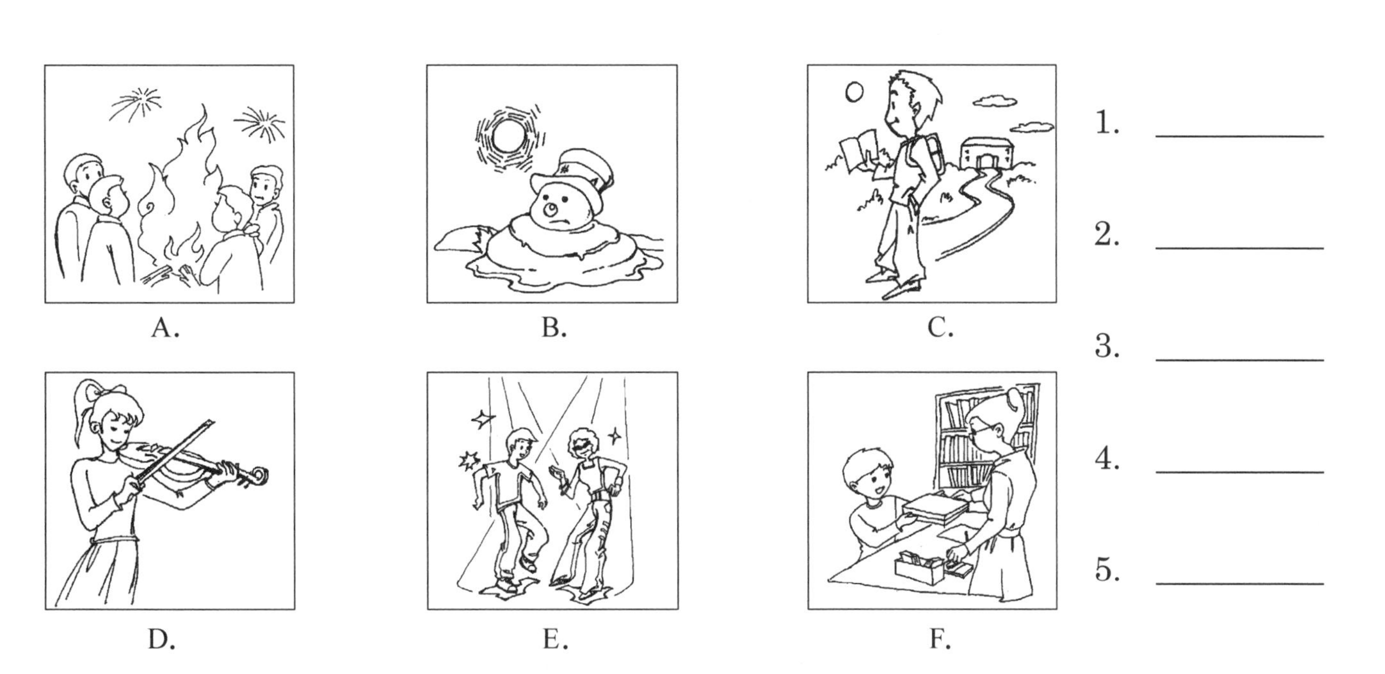

1. ________
2. ________
3. ________
4. ________
5. ________

Ⅱ、Listen and choose the right word you hear in each sentence.（根據你所聽到的句子，選出正確的單字。）（5分）

(　) 6. (A)plane (B)plan (C)play (D)pilot

(　) 7. (A)sheep (B)ship (C)drop (D)trip

(　) 8. (A)bay (B)buy (C)by (D)bye

(　) 9. (A)cast (B)coast (C)cost (D)coat

(　) 10. (A)son (B)soon (C)sun (D)so

Ⅲ、Listen and choose the best response to the sentence you hear.（根據你所聽到句子，選出最恰當的應答句。）（5分）

(　) 11. (A)I have seen a lot of beautiful beaches.
(B)I live near Sandy Bay, but far away from Happy Town.

(C)I don't live in Garden City.

(D)I have been to Space Museum in Moon Town.

(　) 12. (A)Yes, it's near Spring Bay.

(B)No, it's far away from Spring Bay.

(C)It's far away from Spring Bay.

(D)It's near Sandy Bay.

(　) 13. (A)That's a good idea. (B)That's all right.

(C)Thank you. (D)It's a good time.

(　) 14. (A)Ten yuan. (B)Let's go by bus.

(C)What about next Friday? (D)All right.

(　) 15. Thank you, Tom. Can you help me take these exercise books to your classroom?

(B)I don't think so. You can go back to your classroom now.

(C)Can you help me, Tom?

(D)That's all right. You must do your homework now.

Ⅳ、Listen to the dialogue and choose the best answer to the question you hear. （根據你所聽到的對話和問題，選出最恰當的答案。）（5分）

(　) 16. (A)Her sister.

(B)Her father.

(C)Her mother.

(D)Her father and mother.

(　) 17. (A)He was playing a game with his friend.

(B)He was talking to his friend.

(C)He was playing a game with his cousin.

(D)He was talking with his cousin.

(　) 18. (A)At 7 a.m. (B)At 9 a.m. (C)At 10 a.m. (D)At 11 a.m.

(　) 19. (A)35 yuan. (B)30 yuan. (C)25 yuan. (D)45 yuan.

(　) 20. (A)In the supermarket. (B)In the park.

(C)In the shopping centre. (D)In the museum.

V 、Listen to the passage and decide whether the following statements are True (T) or False (F). (判斷下列句子內容是否符合你所聽到的短文內容，符合的用 T 表示，不符合的用 F 表示。) (5 分)

(　) 21. Mike, Jane and Jim are planning some activities for their winter holidays.
(　) 22. Mike's parents live in Beijing and he would like to see them there.
(　) 23. Jane would like to read some science fiction during the holidays.
(　) 24. Jim won't live in their old flat and he will move into a new one.
(　) 25. Jim thinks that Shanghai Students' Post is helpful to his study.

VI 、Listen to the dialogue and choose the activities Ally will do today, tomorrow and the day after tomorrow. (根據你所聽到的對話內容，為 Ally 選出她今天、明天及後天將要做的事情。) (5 分)

Things Ally will do today C __26__

Things Ally will do tomorrow __27__ __28__

Things Ally will do the day after tomorrow __29__ __30__

Activities

(A) cook for her grandparents　　(B)study for a test
(C)go to the doctor's　　(D)take a piano lesson
(E) have a basketball match　　(F) look after her baby sister

26. ________　27. ________　28. ________
29. ________　30. ________

全新國中會考英語聽力精選(上)

Unit 4

I、Listen and choose the right picture.（根據你所聽到的內容，選出相應的圖片。）（6分）

A. B. C.

D. E. F. G.

1. ________ 2. ________ 3. ________

4. ________ 5. ________ 6. ________

II、Listen and choose the best response to the sentence you hear.（根據你所聽到的句子，選出最恰當的應答句。）（6分）

(　) 7. (A)He draws pictures of different places.
(B)He draws plans of tall buildings.
(C)He keeps our city safe and catches thieves.
(D)He makes sick people better and looks after them.

(　) 8. (A)In an office in the city centre.
(B)By underground.
(C)At eight in the morning.
(D)I have no interest about it.

( ) 9. (A)I have been a secretary for two years.
(B)I go to work on foot every day.
(C)I take notes and answer phones every day.
(D)I think it's interesting and I get on well with the people in my office.

( ) 10. (A)He had an accident. (B)He went to school.
(C)He will move to a new flat. (D)He goes there by car.

( ) 11. (A)I see many people buying newspapers from newspaper sellers.
(B)I usually meet my teacher on the way.
(C)I have some coffee and bread on the way to school.
(D)I don't want to see anything on the way.

( ) 12. (A)The doctor and the nurse. (B)The policeman.
(C)The ambulance man. (D)The SPCA officer.

Ⅲ、Listen to the dialogue and choose the best answer to the question you hear.
(根據你所聽到的對話和問題，選出最恰當的答案。)(6分)

( ) 13. (A)English and French. (B)English and German.
(C)English and Chinese. (D)English.

( ) 14. (A)At school. (B)At home.
(C)In a restaurant. (D)In the hospital.

( ) 15. (A)She wants her to go to bed early.
(B)She wants her to go shopping with them.
(C)She wants her not to make any noise.
(D)She wants her to answer a phone call.

( ) 16. (A)She's too busy. (B)She is seeing a film.
(C)She's too tired. (D)She has something to do.

( ) 17. (A)He's going to work to get some working experiences.
(B)He's going to travel by air.
(C)He has found a good job.
(D)He has got many experiences.

( ) 18. (A)In her home. (B)In the teachers' office.
(C)On the playground. (D)On her bike.

IV、Listen to the passage and decide whether the following statements are True (T) or False (F). (判斷下列句子內容是否符合你所聽到的短文內容，符合的用"T" 表示，不符合的用"F" 表示。)(6分)

(　) 19. Susan likes the film very much.

(　) 20. Susan knows the man next to her.

(　) 21. The man is looking for the chocolate, because it's Susan's.

(　) 22. Susan gets angry, because she can't watch the film.

(　) 23. The man doesn't want to find the chocolate on the floor.

(　) 24. In fact, the man is looking for his teeth.

V、Listen and fill in the blanks. (根據你所聽到的內容，用適當的單詞完成下面的句子。每空格限填一詞。)(6分)

- Peter was __25__ years old.
- Peter was interested in __26__.
- Peter thought he would like to find a job and then he could __27__ some money to buy books.
- Peter's first job was to send __28__ to many houses.
- The boss told Peter that the next year he would make __29__ dollars an hour.
- Peter said to the boss, "I will see you __30__ year."

25.__________　　26. __________　　27. __________

28.__________　　29. __________　　30. __________

全新國中會考英語聽力精選(上)

Unit 5

I、Listen and choose the right picture.(根據你所聽到的內容，選出相應的圖片。)(6分)

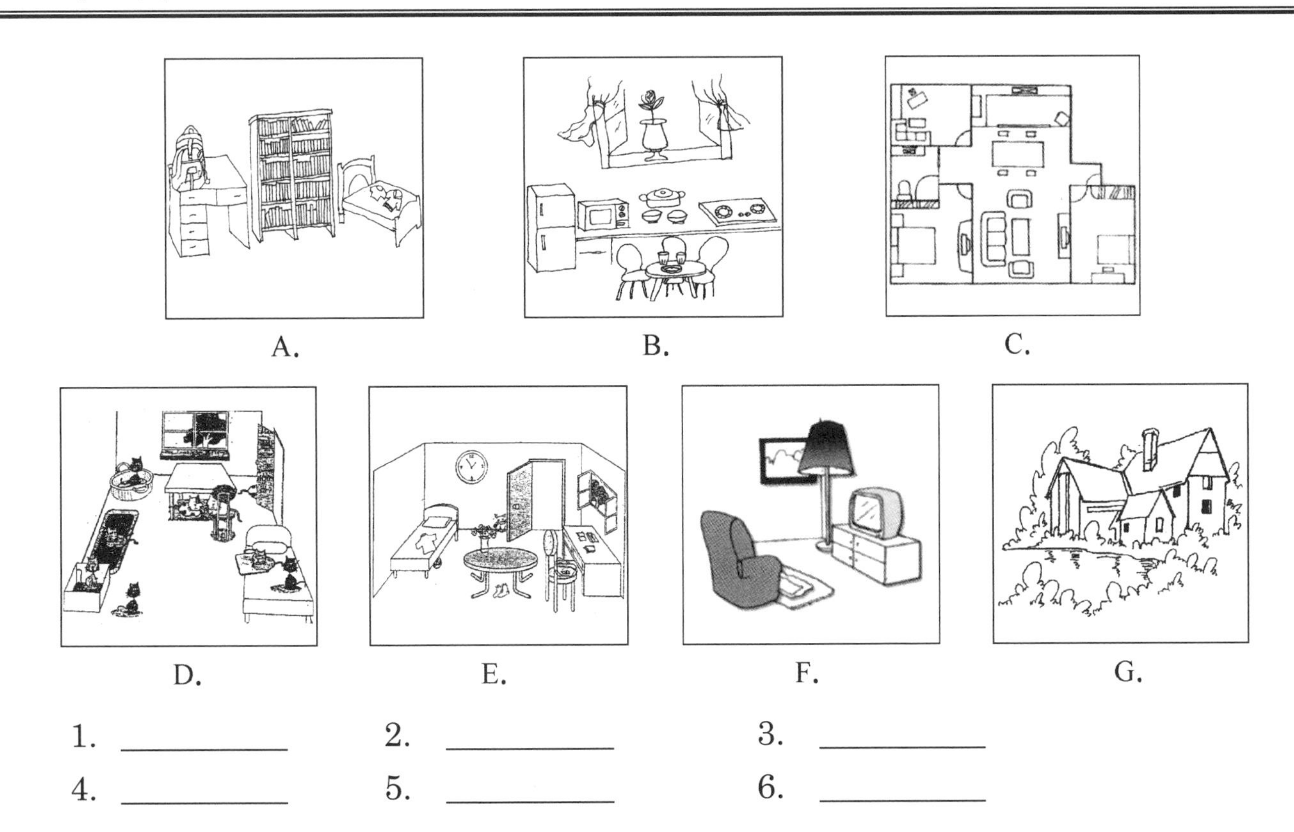

A. B. C. D. E. F. G.

1. ________ 2. ________ 3. ________

4. ________ 5. ________ 6. ________

II、Listen and choose the best response to the sentence you hear.(根據你所聽到的句子，選出最恰當的應答句。)(6分)

( ) 7. (A)Never mind.
(B)Thank you.
(C)It's OK.
(D)Sorry. I'll clean it now.

( ) 8. (A)I want to look for a bigger flat for my family.
(B)Your office looks very nice.
(C)Thank you for your help.
(D)That's all right. Welcome again.

(　) 9. (A)I live in a flat with three bedrooms and two sitting rooms.
(B)Betty wants a flat with three bedrooms and a big balcony.
(C)You can do some exercise every morning on the balcony, I think.
(D)I'm looking for a flat with two bedrooms, one kitchen and two bathrooms.

(　) 10. (A)It's ￥1,800,000 altogether. (B)Is ￥2,500 enough?
(C)It's ￥2,700 a month. (D)￥25,000 a year. OK?

(　) 11. (A)I like it very much.
(B)I don't like it at all.
(C)It's much bigger than the old one.
(D)The old one is much better.

(　) 12. (A)Yes, it is. (B)No, it wasn't.
(C)Yes, I did. (D)No, I won't.

Ⅲ、Listen to the dialogue and choose the best answer to the question you hear.
(根據你所聽到的對話和問題，選出最恰當的答案。)(6分)

(　) 13. (A)7.10. (B)7.20. (C)7.30. (D)7.50.

(　) 14. (A)Mary. (B)Peter. (C)Dick. (D)Billy.

(　) 15. (A)At home. (B)In the school.
(C)In the hospital. (D)Near the shopping centre.

(　) 16. (A)A worker. (B)A doctor.
(C)A nurse. (D)An engineer.

(　) 17. (A)To do a lot of homework. (B)To go to the flower show.
(C)To watch a football match. (D)To watch TV.

(　) 18. (A)The cross talk. (B)The short play.
(C)The group singing. (D)The recitation.

Ⅳ、Listen to the passage and decide whether the following statements are True (T) or False (F). (判斷下列句子內容是否符合你所聽到的短文內容，符合的用"T" 表示，不符合的用"F" 表示。)(6分)

(　) 19. The Lis are going to help others move into a new flat.

(　　) 20. Li Ming is helping his mother with the suitcases.

(　　) 21. There are at least three bedrooms in the new flat.

(　　) 22. The new flat is near Li Hua's school.

(　　) 23. They can go to other places by car or by underground next year.

(　　) 24. Their new flat is in a quiet and beautiful place.

V、Listen to the dialogue and complete the plan.（根據你所聽到的對話內容，用適當的單詞完成下面的平面圖。）(6 分)

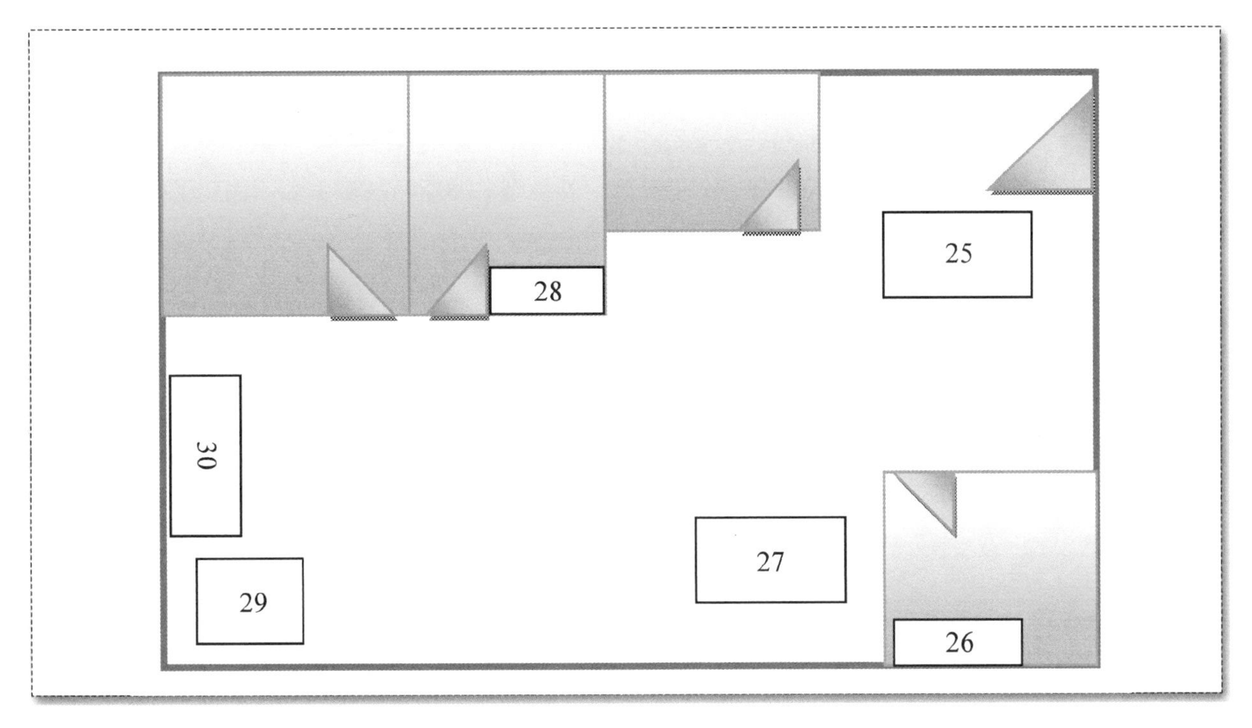

25. ____________　　26. ____________　　27. ____________

28. ____________　　29. ____________　　30. ____________

全新國中會考英語聽力精選(上)

Unit 6

Ⅰ、Listen and choose the right picture.（根據你所聽到的內容，選出相應的圖片）（5分）

A.

B.

C.

D.

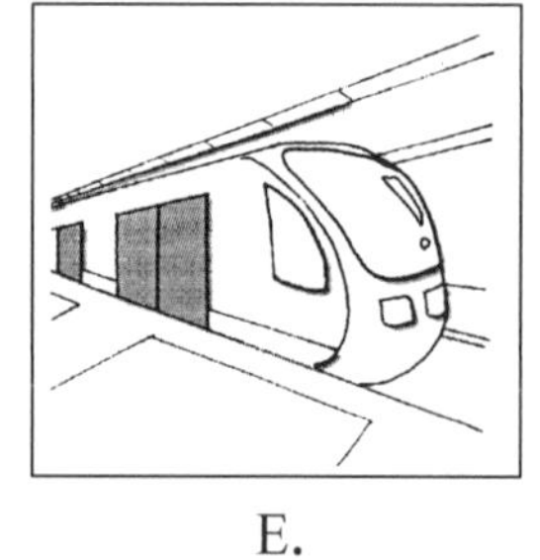

E.

F.

1. ________
2. ________
3. ________
4. ________
5. ________

Ⅱ、Listen and choose the right word you hear in each sentence.（根據你所聽到的句子，選出正確的單字。）（5分）

( ) 6. (A)body (B)bread (C)board (D)boy

( ) 7. (A)children (B)catch (C)church (D)choir

( ) 8. (A)storm (B)store (C)story (D)study

( ) 9. (A)read (B)ready (C)really (D)rainy

( ) 10. (A)minute (B)minus (C)many (D)menu

Ⅲ、Listen and choose the best response to the sentence you hear.（根據你所聽到句子，選出最恰當的應答句。）（5分）

( ) 11. (A)Yes, I live near my school.
(B)No, I live far from my school.

(C)I live near my school.

(D)Sorry, I don't know.

( ) 12. (A)About half an hour. (B)By car.
(C)A long way to go. (D)In five minutes.

( ) 13. (A)I see a post office. (B)By taxi.
(C)A few parents. (D)It takes about an hour.

( ) 14. (A)I see a lot of parents and students, a few teachers and some shops.
(B)I see some books in it.
(C)I can't see anything on the way.
(D)I like walking to school and talking to my friends.

( ) 15. (A)At three fifteen. (B)In the school hall.
(C)At the school entrance. (D)On the second floor.

Ⅳ、Listen to the dialogue and choose the best answer to the question you hear. (根據你所聽到的對話和問題，選出最恰當的答案。)(5分)

( ) 16. (A)By car. (B)By taxi.
(C)By underground. (D)By Maglev.

( ) 17. (A)Parents. (B)Traffic lights. (C)Shops. (D)Restaurants.

( ) 18. (A)5 minutes. (B)10 minutes. (C)20 minutes. (D)30 minutes.

( ) 19. (A)She wants to stay in bed all day.
(B)She wants to visit the boy's home tomorrow.
(C)She wants to have a good time tomorrow.
(D)She wants to have a holiday tomorrow.

( ) 20. (A)She will stay at home.
(B)She will play with Peter's friends in Pudong.
(C)She will catch the underground to People's Square.
(D)I don't know what she will do tomorrow.

Ⅴ、Listen to the passage and decide whether the following statements are True (T) or False (F). (判斷下列句子內容是否符合你所聽到的短文內容，符合的用T表示，不符合的用F表示。)(5分)

( ) 21. Yao Ming plays for Huanghe Football Team.

(　　) 22. The film was made in the USA.

(　　) 23. The film lasts for about one and a half hours.

(　　) 24. You can see Liu Xiang in the film.

(　　) 25. The film can help you know more about Yao Ming.

Ⅵ、Listen to the passage and complete the notice.（根據你所聽到的短文內容，用適當的單詞或數字完成下面的通知。每空格限填一個單詞或數字。）（5 分）

Programme:

- __26__ a.m.： meet at the school gate
- Activities in the park:
  play __27__
  have __28__

sit and chat under the tree

go to the Swimming__29__

- 6 p.m.： go home

Other information:

Ticket price: ￥__30__/child

26.__________　　27. __________　　28. __________

29.__________　　30. __________

全新國中會考英語聽力精選(上)

Unit 7

I、Listen and choose the right picture.(根據你所聽到的內容,選出相應的圖片。)(6分)

1. ________ 2. ________ 3. ________

4. ________ 5. ________ 6. ________

II、Listen and choose the best response to the sentence you hear.(根據你所聽到的句子,選出最恰當的應答句。)(6分)

( ) 7. (A)That sounds great. (B)I don't like any drinks.
(C)Let's have some drinks. (D)Drinks are good for us.

( ) 8. (A)It's November 1. (B)It's autumn.
(C)It's windy and cold. (D)It's eight o'clock.

( ) 9. (A)So is my brother. (B)Neither is my brother.
(C)So does my brother. (D)Neither does my brother.

( ) 10. (A)Hot dogs. (B)Raisin Scones.
(C)Sushi. (D)Rice dumplings.

(　) 11. (A)What a pity! (B)That's a great idea.
(C)What is a food festival? (D)We hold it at school.

(　) 12. (A)I don't know.
(B)The police station is over there.
(C)Walk for two blocks and then turn right.
(D)The police station isn't far.

Ⅲ、Listen to the dialogue and choose the best answer to the question you hear.（根據你所聽到的對話和問題,選出最恰當的答案。）(6分)

(　) 13. (A)On June 13. (B)On July 30.
(C)On June 30. (D)On July 13.

(　) 14. (A)The Spring Festival. (B)Mid-autumn Festival.
(C)Lantern Festival. (D)Dragon Boat Festival.

(　) 15. (A)Once a day. (B)Once a week.
(C)Twice a day. (D)Twice a week.

(　) 16. (A)John doesn't like hot dogs. (B)John likes hot dogs.
(C)The girl will give John a puppy. (D)Eddie will give John a hot dog.

(　) 17. (A)Forty-two. (B)Forty-six.
(C)Sixty-four. (D)Thirty-one.

(　) 18. (A)Spring. (B)Summer.
(C)Autumn. (D)Winter.

Ⅳ、Listen to the dialogue and decide whether the following statements are True (T) or False (F).（判斷下列句子內容是否符合你所聽到的對話內容,符合的用"T"表示,不符合的用"F"表示。）(6分)

(　) 19. Today is Thanksgiving Day.

(　) 20. Jenny and her father went to her grandparents' home in the evening.

(　) 21. Jenny's grandmother cooked a turkey for them.

(　) 22. Jenny's grandmother made some apple pies.

(　) 23. Tom was playing with his toy horse when Jenny saw him.

(　) 24. After the meal, Jenny and her father still stayed there.

V、Listen and fill in the blanks.（根據你所聽到的內容,用適當的單詞完成下面的句子。每空格限填一詞。）（6分）

25. Japanese food is getting more and more ___________.

26. The most ___________ Japanese food is sushi, which you can buy in the supermarkets all around the world.

27. It's ___________ to eat in the restaurants.

28. You can save a lot of money by ___________ it yourself. And it's easy. There are lots of different ways of making sushi. Here is one way.

29. Put some _________, salt and vinegar in a cup.

30. Cut the salmon into, then press the salmon on top of the rice balls ___________.

全新國中會考英語聽力精選(上)

Unit 8

Ⅰ、Listen and choose the right picture.（根據你所聽到的內容，選出相應的圖片。）（6 分）

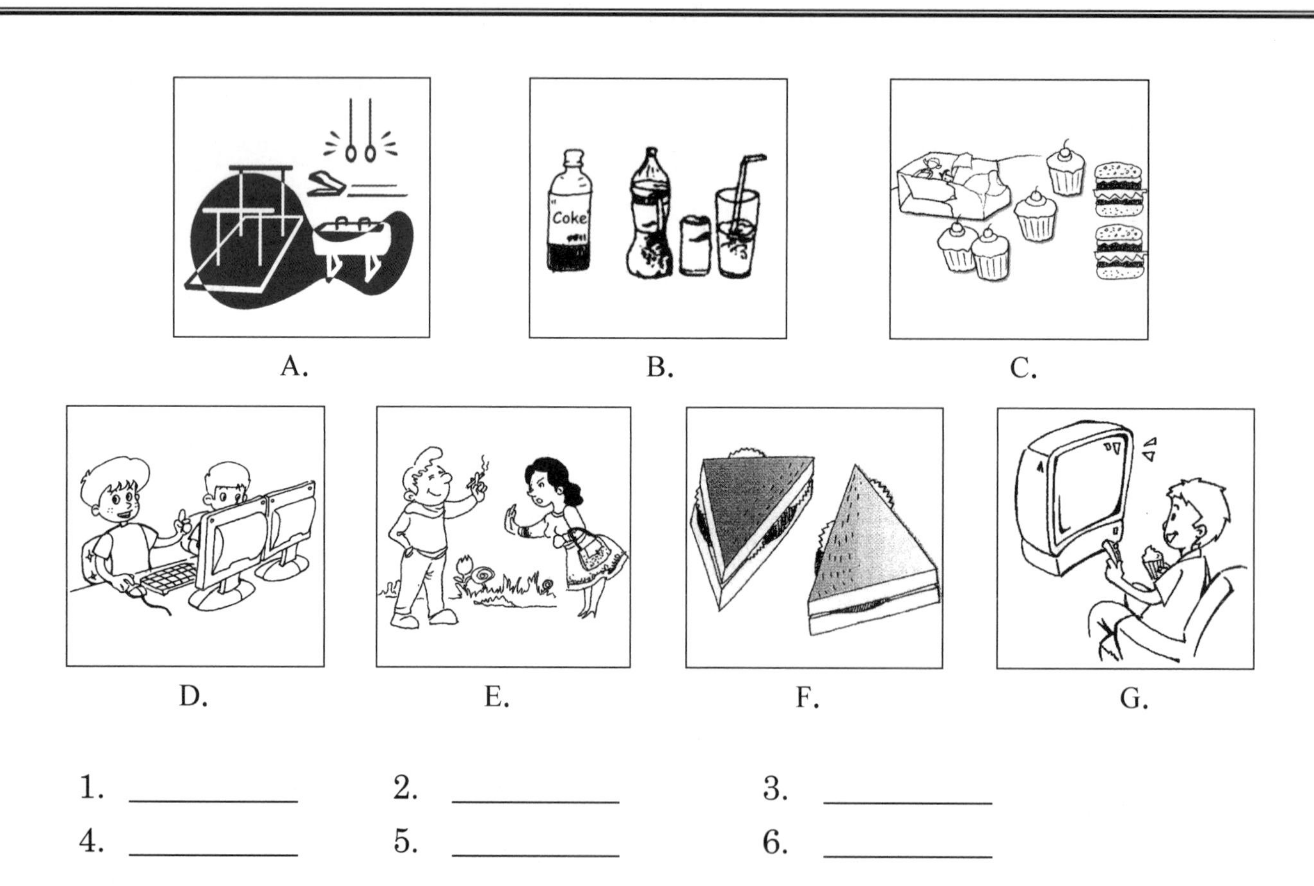

A.　B.　C.

D.　E.　F.　G.

1. ________　2. ________　3. ________

4. ________　5. ________　6. ________

Ⅱ、Listen and choose the best response to the sentence you hear.（根據你所聽到的句子，選出最恰當的應答句。）（6 分）

(　) 7. (A)So have I.
(B)Neither have I.
(C)So do I.
(D)Neither do I.

(　) 8. (A)Thank you very much.
(B)I'm afraid I can't go with you. I have something important to do.
(C)It's very kind of you.
(D)I'm very sorry to tell you that the water is very dirty.

(　) 9. (A)We should eat more sweets and fewer vegetables.
(B)We should exercise regularly.
(C)We don't need to get up very early.
(D)We must follow our teacher's advice.

(　) 10. (A)You will need to drink a lot of water.
(B)You may get fat.
(C)You must give up the habit of eating too much sweets.
(D)You need to go to the gym.

(　) 11. (A)Really? (B)I'm sorry to hear that.
(C)Do you feel much better now? (D)Why do you come here?

(　) 12. (A)It doesn't matter much.
(B)Do you know about it?
(C)You should change your bad habits.
(D)It's OK.

Ⅲ、Listen to the dialogue and choose the best answer to the question you hear.（根據你所聽到的對話和問題，選出最恰當的答案。）(6分)

(　) 13. (A)In the school canteen. (B)In the library.
(C)In a bookshop. (D)On the playground.

(　) 14. (A)Red. (B)White.
(C)Green. (D)Black.

(　) 15. (A)Seven. (B)Eight.
(C)Nine. (D)Ten.

(　) 16. (A)Ten years old. (B)Twelve years old.
(C)Fifteen years old. (D)Eight years old.

(　) 17. (A)In the USA. (B)In Paris. (C)In New York. (D)In Australia.

(　) 18. (A)He has toothache. (B)He has just got up.
(C)He doesn't like sweet food. (D)He has to go to bed.

Ⅳ、Listen to the passage and decide whether the following statements are True (T) or False (F).（判斷下列句子內容是否符合你所聽到的短文內容，符合的用"T" 表示，不符合的用"F" 表示。）(6分)

(　) 19. The manager was having a talk with a young man.

(　) 20. The young man and the manager are friends.

(　) 21. The manager was surprised because the young man asked for a lot of money, but he could almost do nothing.

(　) 22. The manager thought that the workers in the factory should get the same pay.

(　) 23. The young man said he should be better paid because he would work harder than others.

(　) 24. The manager won't employ the young man.

V、Listen to the dialogue and complete the table.（根據你所聽到的對話內容，用適當的單詞完成下面的表格。每空格限填一詞。）（6 分）

	BEFORE	NOW
FOOD	junk food like __25__ chicken and __26__	__27__ fruit and vegetables, more __28__ than meat
DRINK	__29__ drinks	__30__ and fruit juice

25.__________　　26. __________　　27. __________

28.__________　　29. __________　　30. __________

全新國中會考英語聽力精選(上)

Unit 9

Ⅰ、Listen and choose the right picture.（根據你所聽到的內容，選出相應的圖片）（5 分）

A.

B.

C.

D.

E.

F.

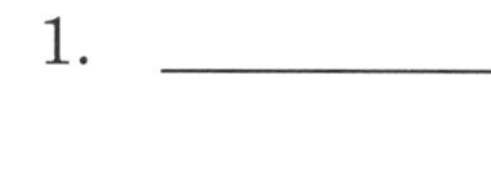

1. ________
2. ________
3. ________
4. ________
5. ________

Ⅱ、Listen and choose the right word you hear in each sentence.（根據你所聽到的句子，選出正確的單字。）（5 分）

(　) 6. (A)snake　(B)snail　(C)stall　(D)snack

(　) 7. (A)she　(B)short　(C)shall　(D)sheet

(　) 8. (A)will　(B)wing　(C)win　(D)wish

(　) 9. (A)spicy　(B)speak　(C)sport　(D)special

(　) 10. (A)better　(B)bitter　(C)bit　(D)biscuit

Ⅲ、Listen and choose the best response to the sentence you hear.（根據你所聽到的句子，選出最恰當的應答句。）（5 分）

(　) 11. (A)It's Friday today.　(B)It's 2 May today.
(C)It's windy today.　(D)On Saturday afternoon.

(　) 12. (A)No, thanks. (B)OK. Here you are.
(C)It's all right. (D)That's a good idea.

(　) 13. (A)OK. That's a good idea. (B)Me too.
(C)Shall we? (D)Thank you.

(　) 14. (A)At the meat section. (B)At the vegetable section.
(C)At the fruit section. (D)At the seafood section.

(　) 15. (A)Yes. Here we are. (B)No, thanks.
(C)That's all right. (D)Nice to meet you.

Ⅳ、Listen to the dialogue and choose the best answer to the question you hear.（根據你所聽到的對話和問題，選出最恰當的答案。）(5 分)

(　) 16. (A)Because he has eaten too much. (B)Because there is none at home.
(C)Because it's time to go to bed. (D)Because his mother is out.

(　) 17. (A)Yes, she does. (B)No, she doesn't.
(C)Yes, he does. (D)No, he doesn't.

(　) 18. (A)Friday. (B)Saturday. (C)Sunday. (D)Monday.

(　) 19. (A)She's doing the housework.
(B)She's helping her son with his homework.
(C)He's doing his homework.
(D)He's helping his mother with the housework.

(　) 20. (A)It open at 9.30 a.m. (B)It closes at 9.15 p.m.
(C)It opens at 8.30 a.m. (D)It closes at 8.45 p.m.

Ⅴ、Listen to the passage and decide whether the following statements are True (T) or False (F).（判斷下列句子內容是否符合你所聽到的短文內容，符合的用 T 表示，不符合的用 F 表示。）(5 分)

(　) 21. All Chinese people like to have fruit after dinner.
(　) 22. British people eat a lot of fresh vegetables.
(　) 23. British people usually have ice cream after meals.
(　) 24. British people like to have a picnic in the garden.
(　) 25. Hamburgers are the cheapest fast food in America.

Ⅵ、Listen to the passage and complete the notes.（根據你所聽到的短文內容，用適當的單詞或數字完成下面的筆記。每空格限填一個單詞或數字。）（5分）

Shopping: Who? __26__ Where? Rose __27__ Supermarket When? On __28__ Cooking:	Who? Mother What? __29__ sausages fruit __30__ When? At weekends

26.__________ 27. __________ 28. __________
29.__________ 30. __________

全新國中會考英語聽力精選(上)

Unit 10

Ⅰ、Listen and choose the right picture.（根據你所聽到的內容，選出相應的圖片）（5分）

A.

B.

C.

D.

E.

F.

1. ________
2. ________
3. ________
4. ________
5. ________

Ⅱ、Listen and choose the right word you hear in each sentence.（根據你所聽到的句子，選出正確的單字。）（5分）

(　) 6. (A)litter (B)list (C)letter (D)little

(　) 7. (A)food (B)foot (C)fruit (D)for

(　) 8. (A)country (B)cousin (C)cool (D)cut

(　) 9. (A)week (B)word (C)let (D)wet

(　) 10. (A)night (B)light (C)right (D)height

Ⅲ、Listen and choose the best response to the sentence you hear.（根據你所聽到的句子，選出最恰當的應答句。）（5分）

(　) 11. (A)Fine, thanks. (B)Good. (C)All right. (D)No, I can't.

(　　) 12. (A)I'm sorry. I'll turn it down. (B)What?
(C)No, I'm watching TV. (D)My pleasure.

(　　) 13. (A)Yes, it is. (B)No, it isn't. (C)Of course. (D)Yes, you are.

(　　) 14. (A)It's five. (B)It's over there. (C)It's five yuan. (D)It's your ball.

(　　) 15. (A)Yes, they are. (B)Yes, there are. (C)No, they aren't. (D)OK.

Ⅳ、Listen to the dialogue and choose the best answer to the question you hear. (根據你所聽到的對話和問題，選出最恰當的答案。)(5 分)

(　　) 16. (A)5.00 a.m. (B)5.30 a.m. (C)6.00 a.m. (D)6.30 a.m.

(　　) 17. (A)Ben. (B)Ben's sister.
(C)Ben's brother. (D)Ben and his sister.

(　　) 18. (A)14. (B)8. (C)22. (D)6.

(　　) 19. (A)Yes, he can. (B)No, he can't.
(C)Yes, he does. (D)No, he doesn't.

(　　) 20. (A)Play table tennis. (B)Do his homework.
(C)Help his mother. (D)Play tennis.

Ⅴ、Listen to the passage and decide whether the following statements are True (T) or False (F). (判斷下列句子內容是否符合你所聽到的短文內容，符合的用 T 表示，不符合的用 F 表示。)(5 分)

(　　) 21. When Jeff was young, he was fat and unhealthy.

(　　) 22. Jeff's friend suggested he go to work by car.

(　　) 23. Jeff bought a new bicycle from a market.

(　　) 24. Jeff would be healthy and strong again because he did some exercise every day.

(　　) 25. Riding a bicycle can help people keep fit.

Ⅵ、Listen and fill in the blanks. (根據你所聽到的內容，用適當的單詞完成下面的句子。每空格限填一個單詞。)(5 分)

- Alice is __26__ years old.
- Alice usually has some milk, some pieces of __27__ for breakfast.

- Alice usually has noodles, a little meat and some fruit __28__ for lunch.
- Alice usually has some rice, fish and vegetable __29__ for dinner.
- Alice's diet is__30__.

26.__________ 27. __________ 28. __________

29.__________ 30. __________

全新國中會考英語聽力精選(上)

Unit 11

I 、Listen and choose the right picture.（根據你所聽到的內容,選出相應的圖片。）（6 分）

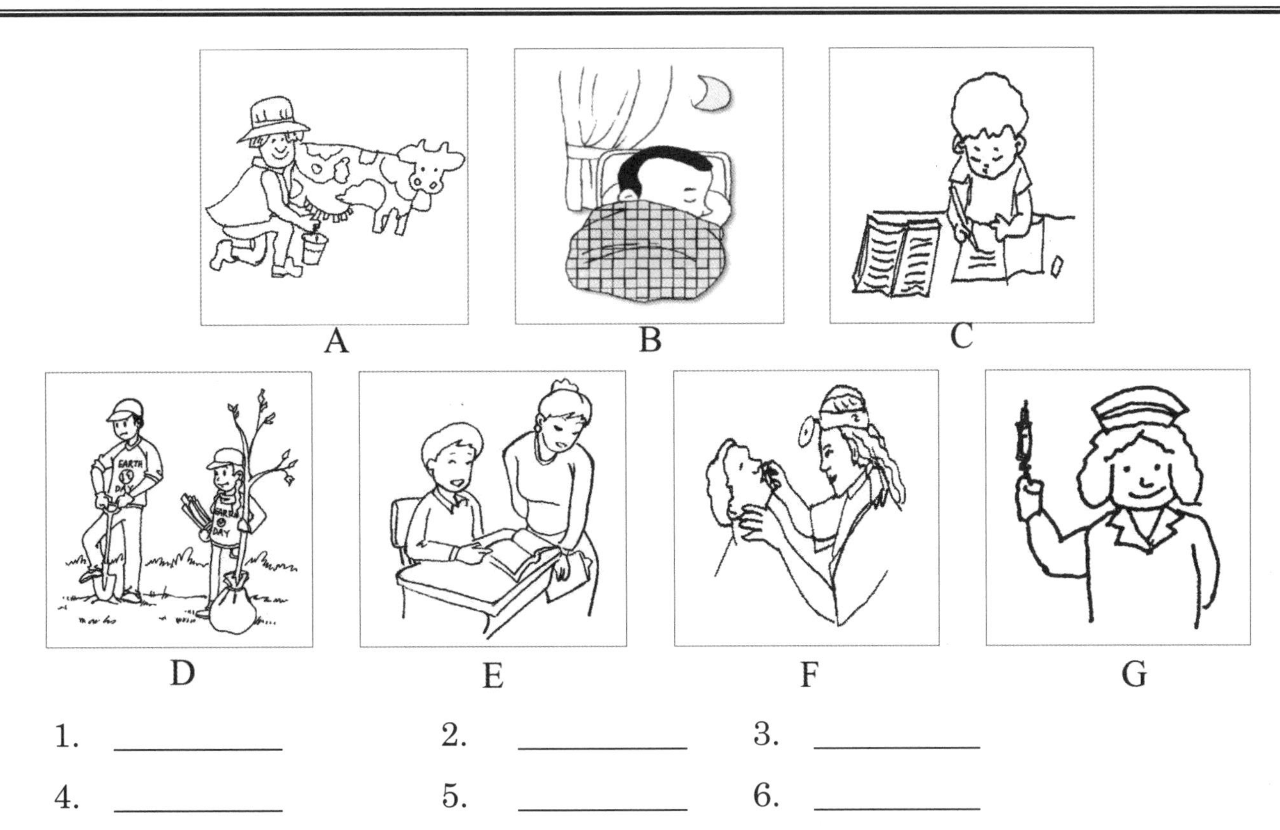

1. ________ 2. ________ 3. ________

4. ________ 5. ________ 6. ________

II 、Listen and choose the best response to the sentence you hear.（根據你所聽到的句子,選出最恰當的應答句。）（6 分）

( ) 7. (A)To the library. (B)This Sunday. (C)At 3 o'clock. (D)Once a week.

( ) 8. (A)I'm glad you like it. (B)It's good. (C)Yes, it is. (D)I'm sorry to hear that.

( ) 9. (A)That's all right. (B)You are welcome. (C)Thank you for your advice. (D)No, I won't.

( ) 10. (A)I have got a bad cold.
(B)I will go to the park tomorrow.
(C)I am doing my homework.
(D)There is something wrong with me.

( ) 11. (A)So can I. (B)Neither can I.
(C)So can't I. (D)Neither can't I.

( ) 12. (A)Much better. Thank you. (B)I'm better. Thanks.
(C)He's writing a report. (D)You are so kind.

Ⅲ、Listen to the dialogue and choose the best answer to the question you hear.(根據你所聽到的對話和問題,選出最恰當的答案。)(6分)

( ) 13. (A)At the cinema. (B)On the school playground.
(C)At the clinic. (D)In the hospital.

( ) 14. (A)A teacher. (B)A reporter.
(C)A doctor. (D)A scientist.

( ) 15. (A)At 6. (B)At 7.
(C)At 6:30. (D)At 7:30.

( ) 16. (A)It will be rainy. (B)It will be cloudy.
(C)It will be snowy. (D)It will be windy.

( ) 17. (A)Lily. (B)Peter.
(C)Tom. (D)Jack.

( ) 18. (A)Milk. (B)Bread.
(C)Pizza. (D)Noodles.

Ⅳ、Listen to the dialogue and decide whether the following statements are True (T) or False (F).(判斷下列句子內容是否符合你所聽到的對話內容,符合的用"T"表示,不符合的用"F"表示。)(6分)

( ) 19. Jimmy is good at all his subjects.

( ) 20. Jimmy always does a lot of math problems.

( ) 21. It takes Kitty about 40 minutes to get to school.

( ) 22. Kitty takes a bus first and then she takes the underground.

( ) 23. Tom couldn't answer his brother's question.

( ) 24. Tom is a model student now.

V、Listen and fill in the blanks.(根據你所聽到的內容,用適當的單詞完成下面的句子。每空格限填一詞。)(6分)

Dear Alice,

12 __25__ is my birthday. I'd like to __26__ you to my birthday party. The party will __27__ at 6 p.m. at my flat. Many of our friends are coming. We are going to have a __28__ in the garden. We are also going to sing karaoke. We'll watch __29__, too. I hope you will be __30__ that day. See you then.

Yours,
Jenny

全新國中會考英語聽力精選(上)

Unit 12

Ⅰ、Listen and choose the right picture.（根據你所聽到的內容,選出相應的圖片。）（6分）

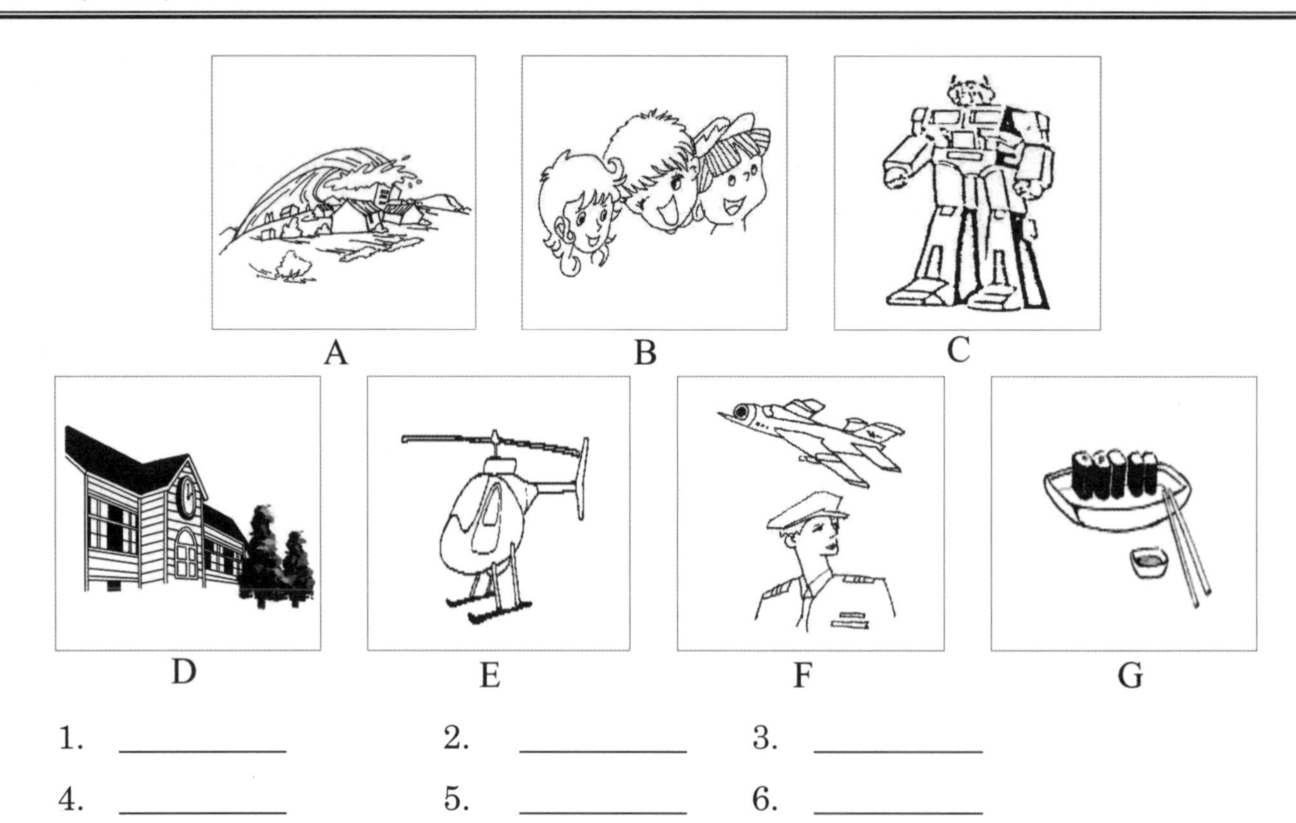

1. ________　2. ________　3. ________

4. ________　5. ________　6. ________

Ⅱ、Listen and choose the best response to the sentence you hear.（根據你所聽到的句子,選出最恰當的應答句。）（6分）

(　) 7. (A)I think not. (B)I think so, too.
(C)Yes, I do. (D)So will we.

(　) 8. (A)How much are the tomatoes? (B)OK. Ten yuan, please.
(C)The tomatoes are fresh. (D)At the market.

(　) 9. (A)You are welcome.
(B)Never mind. Take care next time.
(C)All right.
(D)Here you are.

(　) 10. (A)Would you like to come to my party?
(B)Come to my party.
(C)My party is great.
(D)You must come to my party.

(　) 11. (A)In the morning. (B)In Japan.
(C)In April. (D)It is Sunday.

(　) 12. (A)Yes, I can. (B)No, I can't.
(C)With pleasure. (D)Thank you.

Ⅲ、Listen to the dialogue and choose the best answer to the question you hear.（根據你所聽到的對話和問題,選出最恰當的答案。）（6 分）

(　) 13. (A)Action films. (B)Funny films.
(C)Documentaries. (D)Love stories.

(　) 14. (A)120 yuan. (B)150 yuan.
(C)270 yuan. (D)300 yuan.

(　) 15. (A)On foot. (B)By bike.
(C)By bus. (D)By taxi.

(　) 16. (A)Shanghai Zoo. (B)Dongping National Forest Park.
(C)Changfeng Park. (D)Nanjing Road.

(　) 17. (A)Spring. (B)Summer. (C)Autumn. (D)Winter.

(　) 18. (A)Green. (B)Yellow. (C)Blue. (D)Black.

Ⅳ、Listen to the dialogue and decide whether the following statements are True (T) or False (F).（判斷下列句子內容是否符合你所聽到的對話內容,符合的用"T"表示,不符合的用"F"表示。）（6 分）

(　) 19. In the year 2015, there will be different kinds of materials for clothes.

(　) 20. The special clothes will easily get dirty.

(　) 21. Because of the special clothes, we will save water and money.

(　) 22. Children need to wear uniforms at school every day in 2050.

(　) 23. Children will stay at home and learn things by computer.

(　) 24. According to the writer, children will be able to design their favorite clothes.

V、Listen and fill in the blanks.（根據你所聽到的內容,用適當的單詞完成下面的句子。每空格限填一詞。）(6 分)

25. Tina looks ___________.

26. The ___________ in some parts of the world will keep dropping.

27. And there will be heavy snowstorm and floods ___________.

28. Although there is terrible air ___________ , Mike thinks we can solve the problem.

29. Perhaps we can move to another ___________ by spacecraft.

30. Let's do something to ___________ the earth from now on.

全新國中會考英語聽力精選(上)

Unit 13

Ⅰ、Listen and choose the right picture.（根據你所聽到的內容，選出相應的圖片）（5 分）

A.

B.

C.

D.

E.

F.

1. ＿＿＿＿＿

2. ＿＿＿＿＿

3. ＿＿＿＿＿

4. ＿＿＿＿＿

5. ＿＿＿＿＿

Ⅱ、Listen and choose the right word you hear in each sentence.（根據你所聽到的句子，選出正確的單字。）（5 分）

(　) 6.	(A)rice	(B)race	(C)right	(D)rose
(　) 7.	(A)sad	(B)said	(C)side	(D)seed
(　) 8.	(A)sun	(B)son	(C)some	(D)so
(　) 9.	(A)greet	(B)great	(C)grand	(D)read
(　) 10.	(A)kid	(B)kite	(C)cat	(D)kind

Ⅲ、Listen and choose the best response to the sentence you hear.（根據你所聽到的句子，選出最恰當的應答句。）（5 分）

(　) 11. (A)Yes, I want.　(B)Sorry, I can't.　(C)Yes, I do.　(D)No, it isn't.

(　) 12. (A)Welcome, please. (B)All right.
(C)Yes, please. (D)You're welcome.

(　) 13. (A)It's Friday. (B)It's seven.
(C)It's fine. (D)It's 10 October.

(　) 14. (A)He's well. Thank you. (B)He's doing some shopping.
(C)He's Mike. (D)He's a maths teacher.

(　) 15. (A)Yes, you can. (B)No, I'm busy. (C)I'm sorry. (D)OK.

Ⅳ、Listen to the dialogue and choose the best answer to the question you hear.（根據你所聽到的對話和問題，選出最恰當的答案。）(5 分)

(　) 16. (A)1 October. (B)4 October. (C)1 July. (D)4 July.

(　) 17. (A)On New Year's Day. (B)On 2 January.
(C)Before New Year's Day. (D)In November.

(　) 18. (A)A tie. (B)A watch.
(C)A pair of sunglasses. (D)A book.

(　) 19. (A)To see a film. (B)To do some shopping.
(C)To visit the museum. (D)To have dinner with her friend.

(　) 20. (A)29 October. (B)29 September. (C)1 October. (D)1 November.

Ⅴ、Listen to the passage and decide whether the following statements are True (T) or False (F).（判斷下列句子內容是否符合你所聽到的短文內容，符合的用 T 表示，不符合的用 F 表示。）(5 分)

(　) 21. The Chinese New Year's Day usually comes in February.

(　) 22. Li Hong usually helps her parents clean the house when the festival comes.

(　) 23. Li Hong likes eating dumplings very much.

(　) 24. Wang Hai enjoys eating New Year's cakes very much.

(　) 25. People always go to restaurants to eat New Year's cakes and dumplings on the festival.

Ⅵ、Listen to the dialogue and complete the table.（根據你所聽到的對話內容，用適當的單詞或數字完成下面的表格。每空格限填一個單詞或數字。）（5 分）

In the morning	Activities	In the afternoon	Activities
8.55 a.m.	An English lesson	1.00 p.m.	English Corner
9.50 a.m.	A __26__ lesson	__29__ p.m.	Students' performances
__27__ a.m.	Headmaster's report	2.35 p.m.	A __30__ between class teachers and parents
12.00 a.m.	__28__		

26. ________　27. ________　28. ________

29. ________　30. ________

全新國中會考英語聽力精選(上)

Unit 14

Ⅰ、Listen and choose the right picture.（根據你所聽到的內容，選出相應的圖片。）（6分）

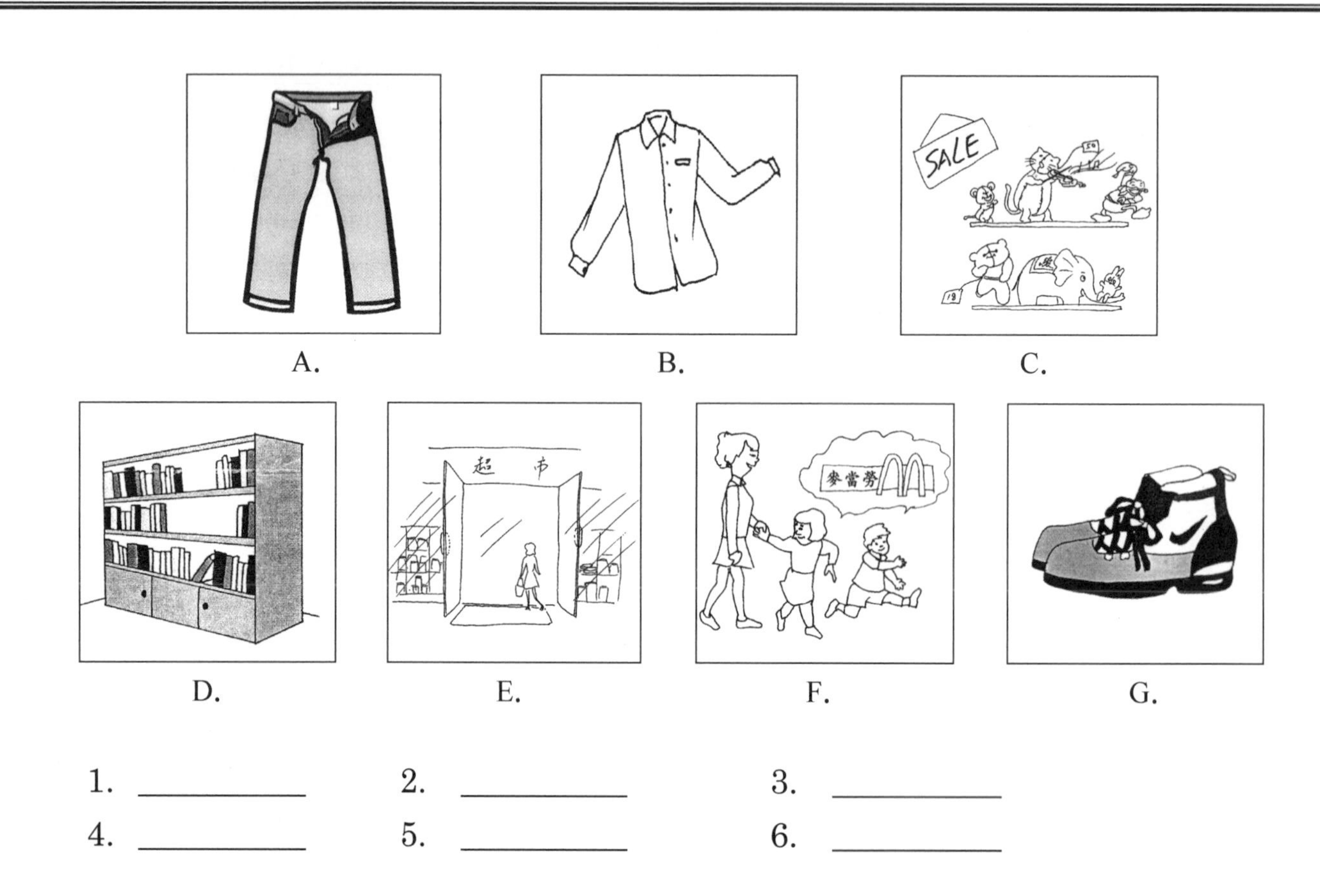

A. B. C. D. E. F. G.

1. ________ 2. ________ 3. ________

4. ________ 5. ________ 6. ________

Ⅱ、Listen and choose the best response to the sentence you hear.（根據你所聽到的句子，選出最恰當的應答句。）（6分）

(　) 7. (A)Certainly. Here you are. (B)No, you mustn't.
(C)Not at all. (D)Yes, I will.

(　) 8. (A)I'm glad you like it. (B)Thank you.
(C)Please don't say so. (D)Of course not.

(　) 9. (A)All right. (B)Of course not.
(C)Never mind. (D)My pleasure.

(　) 10. (A)Sorry to hear that. (B)Please give them three cheers.

(C)Nothing wrong. (D)It's hard to say.

( ) 11. (A)She likes music. (B)She's tall and beautiful.
(C)She is well. (D)She likes me.

( ) 12. (A)That's all right. (B)So do I.
(C)Why not? Let's. (D)Walking is good to you.

Ⅲ、Listen to the dialogue and choose the best answer to the question you hear.（根據你所聽到的對話和問題，選出最恰當的答案。）(6分)

( ) 13. (A)To the playground. (B)To the garden.
(C)To the computer room. (D)To the language laboratory.

( ) 14. (A)On the 1st floor. (B)On the 2nd floor.
(C)On the 4th floor. (D)On the 12th floor.

( ) 15. (A)John and Mary. (B)Mary.
(C)May. (D)John.

( ) 16. (A)A bike. (B)A train. (C)A car. (D)A bus.

( ) 17. (A)At a quarter past six. (B)At six o'clock.
(C)At a quarter to six. (D)At half past six.

( ) 18. (A)On foot. (B)By bike.
(C)By bus. (D)By underground.

Ⅳ、Listen to the passage and decide whether the following statements are True (T) or False (F).（判斷下列句子內容是否符合你所聽到的短文內容，符合的用"T" 表示，不符合的用"F" 表示。）(6分)

( ) 19. George has a wife and a dog.

( ) 20. His car is quite small.

( ) 21. He belongs to a football club.

( ) 22. After his tennis last Monday, his dog did not get into the car with him.

( ) 23. George shouted, and the dog came to him.

( ) 24. The dog was in the right car, and George was in the wrong one.

V、Listen and fill in the blanks.（根據你所聽到的內容，用適當的單詞完成下面的句子。每空格限填一詞。）（6 分）

- An important businessman went to see his doctor because he couldn't __25__ at night.
- The doctor examined him __26__ and asked him if he had any hobbies.
- The businessman __27__ for a while and told the doctor that he didn't have time for hobbies.
- The doctor told him that he didn't have time for anything __28__ his work and he would die in less than __29__ years if he didn't have any hobbies.
- The businessman told the doctor the next day that he had __30__ painted fifteen pictures since he saw the doctor.

25.__________ 26. __________ 27. __________
28.__________ 29. __________ 30. __________

全新國中會考英語聽力精選(上)

Unit 15

Ⅰ、Listen and choose the right picture.(根據你所聽到的內容，選出相應的圖片。)(6分)

1. ________ 2. ________ 3. ________

4. ________ 5. ________ 6. ________

Ⅱ、Listen and choose the best response to the sentence you hear.(根據你所聽到的句子，選出最恰當的應答句。)(6分)

( ) 7. (A)To the park. (B)At the library.
(C)On foot. (D)With my friend.

( ) 8. (A)Let's go. (B)So do I.
(C)Neither do I. (D)Yes, I'd love to.

( ) 9. (A)I like watching TV plays.
(B)The TV play is on Channel 5.
(C)We usually watch TV plays at weekends.

(D)I think so, too.

( ) 10. (A)It's very kind of you. (B)Yes, much better. Thank you.
(C)She works better than before. (D)Yes, I am very well. Thank you.

( ) 11. (A)That's all right. (B)Of course.
(C)OK. I'll take your advice. (D)Never mind.

( ) 12. (A)I'm busy. (B)Yes, please.
(C)Have a great date. (D)Thank you. I'll be glad to come.

Ⅲ、Listen to the dialogue and choose the best answer to the question you hear.
(根據你所聽到的對話和問題，選出最恰當的答案。)(6分)

( ) 13. (A)Six. (B)Five. (C)Only one. (D)Seven.

( ) 14. (A)In 1979. (B)In 1978. (C)In 1980. (D)In 1977.

( ) 15. (A)In a market. (B)In a building. (C)In a library. (D)In a park.

( ) 16. (A)Because he didn't go to bed.
(B)Because he went to bed too late last night.
(C)Because he went to bed early last night.
(D)Because he slept very well.

( ) 17. (A)7 dollars. (B)8 dollars. (C)9 dollars. (D)12 dollars.

( ) 18. (A)France. (B)America. (C)England. (D)Australia.

Ⅳ、Listen to the passage and decide whether the following statements are True (T) or False (F). (判斷下列句子內容是否符合你所聽到的短文內容，符合的用"T" 表示，不符合的用"F" 表示。)(6分)

( ) 19. Kate got a ring as her eighteenth birthday present.

( ) 20. Kate lost the ring outside the kitchen.

( ) 21. Kate was good at making cakes.

( ) 22. Kate's brother found the ring in one of the cakes she had made.

( ) 23. Kate didn't like the ring very much.

( ) 24. Kate decided to make her brother some more cakes for finding the ring.

V、Listen and fill in the blanks. (根據你所聽到的內容，用適當的單詞完成下面的句子。每空格限填一詞。)(6分)

- With the help of programmes of education, children do __25__ in school.
- Children simply watch too much television, so they don't do a lot of other __26__ things for their education.
- When children are watching TV, they are only __27__ to the language, and aren't talking with anyone.
- When school children watch TV, they read __28__.
- All children learn by doing, and they need time to play in order to learn about the __29__.
- At first, stopping watching TV for a month was difficult, but there were soon a lot of good __30__.

25.__________ 26. __________ 27. __________
28.__________ 29. __________ 30. __________

全新國中會考英語聽力精選(上)原文及參考答案

Unit 1

I 、Listen and choose the right picture.（**根據你所聽到的內容,選出相應的圖片。**）（6分）

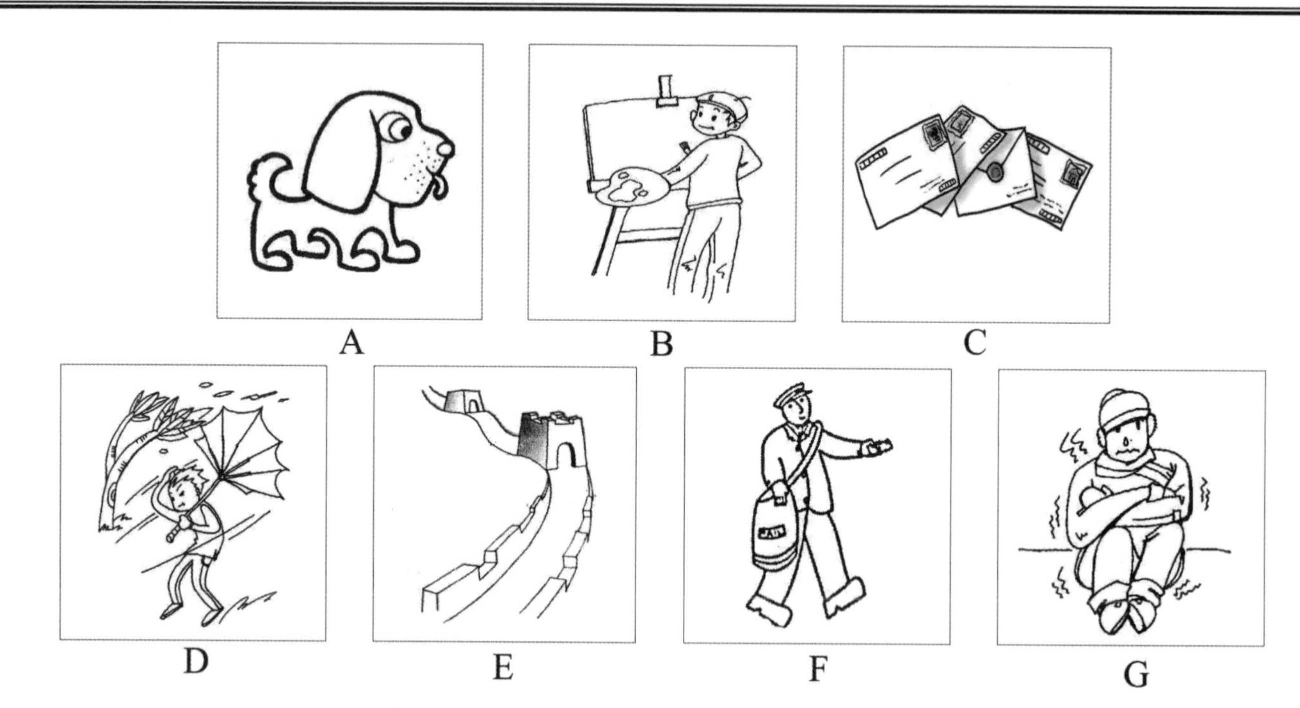

A B C D E F G

1. The wind is blowing so hard that the boy can't walk forwards easily.
（風吹得太強了以至於男孩很難往前走。）
答案：(D)

2. We are going to visit the Great Wall during our stay in Beijing.
（我們待在北京的時候要去參觀萬里長城。）
答案：(E)

3. What a lovely puppy! I hope to have one as my pet, too.
（好可愛的小狗！我也希望有一隻當作我的寵物。）
答案：(A)

4. I've just got some letters from my new pen friend.
（我剛剛收到我新筆友的來信。）
答案：(C)

5. Jack feels so cold now because he has had a cold.
（Jack 現在覺得很冷，因為他已經感冒了。）
答案：(G)

6. My brother's ambition is to be an artist, so he practices drawing every day.
（我哥哥的志向是當藝術家，所以他每天練習作畫。）
答案：(B)

II、Listen and choose the best response to the sentence you hear.（根據你所聽到的句子,選出最恰當的應答句。）(6 分）

7. I couldn't do the math problem. It's too difficult.（我不會做這道數學題。太難了。）
(A)So do I.（我也做。） (B)So could I.（我也會。）
(C)Neither do I.（我也不做。） (D)Neither could I.（我也不會。）
答案：(D)

8. How far is it from the subway station to your school?
（從地鐵站去你的學校有多遠？）
(A)About 10 minutes.（大約十分鐘。） (B)In 10 minutes.（十分鐘之內。）
(C)10-minute walk.（十分鐘的路程。） (D)For 10 minutes.（要十分鐘。）
答案：(C)

9. I've got a terrible headache.（我頭很痛。）
(A)You'd better watch more TV.（你最好多看電視。）
(B)You'd better sleep late.（你最好晚一點睡。）
(C)You'd better sleep earlier.（你最好早一點睡。）
(D)You'd better not go to see the doctor.（你最好不要去看醫生。）
答案：(C)

10. Shall we go to see the film?（我們去看電影好嗎？）
(A)That's a good idea.（好主意。） (B)That's right.（對。）
(C)That's all right.（沒關係。） (D)Of course not.（當然不好。）
答案：(A)

11. Vegetables are good for us.（蔬菜對我們有益。）
(A)I hope so.（我希望如此。） (B)I hope not.（我不希望。）
(C)I agree with you.（我同意。） (D)I don't like.（我不喜歡。）

答案：(C)

12. When will the meeting start?（會議甚麼時候開始？）
(A)At two o'clock.（兩點。） (B)For one hour.（要一個小時。）
(C)In two hours later.（兩小時後。） (D)Two hours.（兩小時。）
答案：(A)

Ⅲ、Listen to the dialogue and choose the best answer to the question you hear.（根據你所聽到的對話和問題,選出最恰當的答案。）(6 分)

13. W: What kind of books have you chosen, James?
（W: James，你挑了哪種書？）
M: Some books on computers. What about you?
（M: 一些電腦書。妳呢？）
W: I want to buy some physics books for my son. Where can I find them?
（W: 我想幫我兒子買一些物理書。我在哪裡可以找到？）
M: On the third floor.（M: 在三樓。）
Q: Where does the dialogue probably take place?（Q: 這段對話大概在哪裡發生？）
(A)In the bookstore.（在書店。）
(B)In the reading room.（在閱覽室。）
(C)In the physics lab.（在物理實驗室。）
(D)In the computer room.（在電腦室。）
答案：(A)

14. W: Why does Jim get up so early?（W: 為什麼 Jim 起這麼早？）
M: Because he works as a newspaper deliverer.
（M: 因為他是送報員。）
Q: Why does Jim get up early?（Q: 為什麼 Jim 起得早？）
(A)Because of the weather.（因為天氣。）
(B)Because of his hobby.（因為他的嗜好。）
(C)Because of his job.（因為他的工作。）
(D)Because of his age.（因為他的年齡。）
答案：(C)

15. W: Look, there's a sign on the wall. What does this sign mean?
（W: 看，牆上有一個標示。這個標示是甚麼意思？）

M: It means we mustn't drink or eat here in the library.
（M: 它的意思是我們不能在圖書館內飲食。）
Q: Where are they speaking?（Q: 他們在哪裡談話？）
(A)In the classroom.（在教室。） (B)In the library.（在圖書館。）
(C)In the hospital.（在醫院。） (D)In the dining room.（在餐廳。）
答案：(B)

16. W: Who studies hardest, Mary, John or Peter?
（W: 誰最努力讀書，Mary、John 還是 Peter？）
M: Well... Mary studies harder than John, but not as hard as Peter.
（M: 嗯...Mary 比 John 努力，但是不像 Peter 那麼努力。）
Q: Who studies hardest?（Q: 誰最努力讀書？）
(A)Mary. (B)Peter. (C)Tom. (D)John.
答案：(B)

17. W: What's the matter with you?（W: 你怎麼了？）
M: I have a headache.（M: 我頭痛。）
W: When did you go to bed last night?（W: 你昨晚幾點睡？）
M: I usually go to bed before ten o'clock. But yesterday I had much work to do and didn't go to bed until midnight.
（M: 我通常十點前就睡了。但是昨天我有太多工作要做，所以一直到半夜才睡。）
Q: When did the man go to bed last night?（Q: 那個男人昨天晚上幾點睡？）
(A)At ten o'clock.（十點。）
(B)Before ten o'clock.（十點之前。）
(C)Before twelve o'clock.（十二點之前。）
(D)At about twelve o'clock.（大約十二點。）
答案：(D)

18. W: Good morning, sir. Can I help you?（W: 先生，早安。我能為你服務嗎？）
M: Yes. I'd like a chicken roll, a green salad and some mushroom soup.
（M: 是的。我想要一個雞肉捲、沙拉、和蘑菇湯。）
W: Something to drink?（W: 要來點喝的嗎？）
M: No, thanks.（M: 不了，謝謝。）
W: A chicken roll, a green salad and some mushroom soup. OK, sir. The food will be ready soon.
（W: 一個雞肉捲、沙拉、和蘑菇湯。好的，先生。餐點馬上就準備好了。）

Q: What is the woman?（Q:那個女人是做甚麼的？）

(A)A secretary.（秘書。）
(B)A waitress.（服務生。）
(C)A librarian.（圖書管理員。）
(D)A shop assistant.（店員。）

答案：(B)

Ⅳ、Listen to the dialogue and decide whether the following statements are True (T) or False (F).（**判斷下列句子內容是否符合你所聽到的對話內容,符合的用"T"表示,不符合的用"F"表示。**）（6分）

Mandy：Hi, Simon. It's wonderful to see you here again!

Mandy：嗨，Simon。真開心又在這裡看到你。

Simon：How was London, Mandy?

Simon：Mandy，倫敦怎麼樣？

Mandy：It was great! There is so much to see and so many things to do! I loved seeing all the different kinds of people there.

Mandy：好棒！有好多可看的，也有好多可做的。在那裡看到各式各樣的人，我愛死了。

Simon：What do you mean by "different kinds of people"？

Simon：「各式各樣的人」是甚麼意思？

Mandy：People from different places. It's fun just to look at all their faces.

Mandy：從各地來的人。光是看他們的臉就很有趣。

Simon：Is London a very big city?

Simon：倫敦是個非常大的城市嗎？

Mandy：Well, yes. It's the biggest city in Europe, and most of the interesting places are near the city centre.

Mandy：是。它是歐洲最大的城市，而且大部分有趣的地方都在市中心附近。

Simon：What did you like best about London?

Simon：妳最喜歡倫敦的甚麼？

Mandy：Well, I loved the buses. We travelled around the city on a double-decker bus every day. I always sat upstairs so that I could see better. We saw the Queen's Palace, though we didn't see the Queen. We also went to a wax museum. It had statues of all the most famous people in the world. I saw one of David Beckham. It looked like a real person. I even saw someone trying to ask a statue a question!

Mandy：我喜歡公車。我們每天搭雙層公車遊覽市區。我總是坐在上層，所以我可以看得更清楚。我們看到女王的皇宮，雖然我們沒看到女王。我們也去了蠟像博物館。那兒有世界上所有知名人士的蠟像。我看到貝克漢的蠟像。看起來好像真人。我甚至看到有人對著蠟像問問題！

Simon：Did you go on the river?

Simon：妳去河上遊覽了嗎？

Mandy：Yes. We sailed down the River Thames in a boat. It was raining, but still it was interesting to see all the famous old bridges. Oh, here's the waiter. Let's order our food, and then I'll show you my photos of China Town.

Mandy：去了。我們搭船在泰晤士河航行。那天正下著雨，但是看到所有知名的古老橋樑還是很有趣。喔，服務生來了。我們來點餐吧，然後我要給你看我在中國城拍的相片。

19. London is the largest city in the world.（倫敦是世界上最大的城市。）

答案：(F 錯)

20. London is very large, so it is difficult to see something interesting in the city centre.（倫敦非常大，所以在市中心很難看到有趣的事。）

答案：(F 錯)

21. Mandy liked the London buses because they went very fast.
（Many 喜歡倫敦公車因為它們開得非常快。）

答案：(F 錯)

22. Mandy saw David Beckham in the museum.（Mandy 在博物館看到貝克漢。）

答案：(F 錯)

23. It was raining when Mandy was on the River Thames.
（當 Mandy 在泰晤士河上的時候正在下雨。）

答案：(T 對)

24. Mandy has brought some photos that she took in China Town with her.
（Mandy 帶了她在中國城拍的相片。）

答案：(T 對)

V、Listen and fill in the blanks.（**根據你所聽到的內容,用適當的單詞完成下面的句子。每空格限填一詞。**）（6分）

Mary was not in good health. She was often ill. She wanted to be healthy but she didn't know what to do. One day, she asked Miss Black how to keep healthy. Miss Black told her, "First, you must look after yourself and then do something necessary for your health. For example, take a walk after supper, do morning exercises, play sports, eat fruit and vegetables, and wash your hands before meals. All of these things are good for your health."

Mary 的健康不大好。她常常生病。她想要健康但是不知道該怎麼做。有一天，她問 Black 小姐該如何保持健康。Black 小姐對她說：「首先，你必須照顧你自己，為你的健康做一些必要的事。例如：晚餐後散步、做晨間體操、做體育運動、吃水果和蔬菜、餐前洗手。以上所有的事都對你的健康有益。」

Miss Black went on, "Remember! Don't do anything bad for your health, like going to school without breakfast, keeping your fingernails long, watching TV too much, reading in the sun, staying up late and so on."

Black 小姐接著說：「要記住！不要做對健康有害的事，像是不吃早餐就去上學、留長指甲、看太多電視、在太陽底下看書、熬夜...等等。」

After that Mary always did as Miss Black told her. She is very healthy now.

在此之後，Mary 總是依照 Black 小姐告訴她的來做。她現在非常健康。

25. Mary was often ill so she wanted to be healthy. But she didn't know what to do.
Mary 常常生病，所以她想要健康。但是她不知道該怎麼做。

26. Miss Black told Mary that she must look after herself and then do something necessary for her health.
Black 小姐告訴 Mary，她必須照顧自己，並且為她的健康做一些必要的事。

27. Mary should do morning exercises and play sports.
Mary 應該做晨間體操和運動。

28. Mary must eat fruit and vegetables and wash hands before meals.
Mary 必須吃水果和蔬菜，餐前要洗手。

29. Mary shouldn't go to school without breakfast in the morning.
Mary 不應該早上沒吃早餐就去上學。

30. Mary shouldn't watch TV too much , read in the sun or stay up late and so on.
Mary 不應該看太多電視、在太陽底下看書、或熬夜...等等。

全新國中會考英語聽力精選(上)原文及參考答案

Unit 2

I、Listen and choose the right picture.（**根據你所聽到的內容，選出相應的圖片。**）（6分）

1. When your puppy is ill, you can take him to a clinic and a vet will look after him.
   （當你的小狗生病的時候，你可以帶他去診所，獸醫會照顧他。）

   答案：(A)

2. Look, your puppy is holding a bone in its mouth.
   （看，你的小狗嘴裡咬著一根骨頭。）

   答案：(C)

3. Lucy, you need to take your puppy to the garden for a walk at least once a day.
   （Lucy，你要至少每天一次帶你的小狗去花園散步。）

   答案：(E)

4. It is nice to play with our pets after school.
   （放學後跟我們的寵物玩真好。）

   答案：(D)

5. Some cruel people don't look after their dogs and drive them away. The poor dogs have to wander in the streets, looking for food.
（有些殘忍的人不照顧他們的狗而且趕走牠們。可憐的狗兒們不得不在街上流浪尋找食物。）
答案：(F)

6. You need to give some biscuits to your puppy and also a bowl for him to drink water from.
（你需要給你的小狗一些餅乾，也要給他一個碗用來飲水。）
答案：(G)

II、Listen and choose the best response to the sentence you hear.（根據你所聽到的句子，選出最恰當的應答句。）（6 分）【第 10 題，你所聽到的 SPCA 是指防止動物虐待協會】

7. How can we hold these little puppies?
（我們該如何抱這些小狗？）
(A)We should do that softly and gently with our two arms.
（我們應該用我們的雙臂輕柔地抱。）
(B)Give them some puppy biscuits to chew every day.
（每天給他們一些小狗餅乾咬。）
(C)Don't hold them in your arms. Stop!
（不要抱在你的懷裡。停止！）
(D)I'm sorry to hear that.
（我很抱歉聽到這件事。）
答案：(A)

8. Which puppy do you prefer?
（你比較喜歡哪一種小狗？）
(A)There are so many puppies here.（這裡有好多小狗。）
(B)The black and white one.（黑白相間的。）
(C)Take them away, please.（請帶走他們。）
(D)Are you sure about them?（關於他們你確定嗎？）
答案：(B)

9. What can dogs do for blind people?
（狗可以為盲人做甚麼？）
(A)They help them catch thieves.（幫助他們抓小偷。）
(B)They help them cross the streets.（協助他們過馬路。）
(C)They help them hunt animals for food.（幫助他們獵捕動物當作食物。）
(D)They help them guide the caves.（協助他們導覽洞穴。）
答案：(B)

10. What do SPCA officers usually do?
（SPCA 官員通常做甚麼？）
(A)They take dogs to people's homes.（他們把狗帶到人們的家裡。）
(B)They take bad people to police stations.（他們帶壞人去警察局。）
(C)They find homeless animals and look after them.
（他們發現無家可歸的動物，照顧他們。）
(D)They promise to make sick animals better.（他們承諾讓生病的動物轉好。）
答案：(C)

11. What do bad people usually do to their dogs?
（壞人通常對他們的狗做甚麼？）
(A)They give their pets a lot of water to drink.（他們給他們的寵物很多水喝。）
(B)They give their pets some bones to chew.（他們給他們的寵物一些骨頭去咬。）
(C)They hold their pets gently and look after them well.
（他們輕柔地抱他們的狗，好好的照顧他們）
(D)They leave their pets in the streets and never take them back.
（他們把他們的寵物留在街上，再也不帶他們回去。）
答案：(D)

12. Did people raise dogs long ago?
（很久以前人們養狗嗎？）
(A)Yes, they did.（是的，他們養。）
(B)No, they didn't.（不，他們不養。）
(C)Yes, they do.（是的，他們養。）
(D)No, they don't.（不，她們不養。）
答案：(A)

Ⅲ、Listen to the dialogue and choose the best answer to the question you hear.
（根據你所聽到的對話和問題，選出最恰當的答案。）（6分）

13. W: What is John wearing today?
（W: John 今天穿甚麼？）
M: He is wearing a white shirt with short sleeves, blue trousers and red sports shoes.
（M: 他穿一件白色短袖襯衫、藍色長褲和紅色運動鞋。）
W: He is so cool.
（W: 他好酷。）
M: Is he? I don't think so.
（M: 是嗎？我不這麼認為。）
Question: What shirt is John wearing?
（問題：John 穿甚麼襯衫？）
(A)A red shirt with long sleeves.（紅色長袖襯衫。）
(B)A white shirt with short sleeves.（白色短袖襯衫。）
(C)A blue shirt with short sleeves.（藍色短袖襯衫。）
(D)A white shirt with long sleeves.（白色長袖襯衫。）
答案：(B)

14. M: What will you be in 15 years' time, Alice?
（M: Alice，十五年後你會當甚麼？）
W: I will possibly be an astronaut. How about you, Fred?
（W: 我可能是太空人。Fred，你呢？）
M: I want to fly the plane in the sky.
（M: 我想在天上駕駛飛機。）
W: That's great!
（W: 太棒了！）
Question: What will Fred be?
（問題：Fred 將會是甚麼？）
(A)A businessman.（商人）
(B)An astronaut.（太空人）
(C)A pilot.（飛行員）

(D)A sportsman.（運動員）

答案：(C)

15. M: Stop walking, Kitty. The red light is on!
（M: Kitty，不要走了。紅燈亮了！）

W: But there are no cars and buses here.
（W: 但是這裡沒有車和公車。）

M: We must obey the traffic rules and try to be lovely Shanghainese.
（M: 我們必須遵守交通規則，試著當可愛的上海人。）

W: I see.
（W: 我知道了。）

Question: Where are they talking?
（問題：他們在哪裡說話？）

(A)On the bus.（公車上。）

(B)In the car.（車裡。）

(C)At the crossing.（斑馬線。）

(D)On the street.（街上。）

答案：(C)

16. W: How about your model house, Mike?
（W: Mike，你的模型屋怎麼樣了？）

M: I haven't finished yet. Could you help me?
（M: 我還沒完成。你能幫我嗎？）

W: No problem.
（W: 沒問題。）

M: Would you please lend me some paint and brushes?
（M: 你能借我一些顏料和刷子嗎？）

W: OK.
（W: 好。）

Question: What does the boy want to do?
（問題：男孩想要做甚麼？）

(A)Paint the walls.（漆牆壁。）

(B)Make tables.（做桌子。）

(C)Make the roof.（造屋頂。）

(D)Decorate the walls.（裝飾牆壁。）

答案：(A)

17. M: Let's go to visit Pudong, Mary.
(M: Mary，我們去造訪浦東吧。）

W: OK. How shall we go?
（W: 好。我們怎麼去好呢？）

M: What about by ferry?
（M: 渡輪怎麼樣？）

W: I'm afraid it's too slow. Why not by underground?
（W: 我擔心太慢了。為什麼不搭地鐵？）

M: It's fast, but we can't see anything on the underground train.
（M: 它很快，但是我們在地鐵上看不到任何東西。）

W: Ah, I've got a good idea. Let's go there through the Sightseeing Tunnel.
（W: 啊，我有個好點子。我們從觀光隧道去那裡吧。）

M: That's a good idea.
（M: 真是個好主意。）

Question: How will they go to Pudong?
（問題：他們將如何去浦東？）

(A)By ferry.（搭渡輪。）

(B)By train.（搭火車。）

(C)By underground.（搭地鐵。）

(D)Through Sightseeing Tunnel.（從觀光隧道。）

答案：(D)

18. W: What a sunny day, Eddie!
(W: Eddy，晴天真好。）

M: Yes, it is. Let's go out for a walk.
（M: 是的。我們出去散步吧！）

W: That's a good idea.
（W: 好主意。）

M: Oh, it's quite warm outside.

(M: 喔，外面相當溫暖。)

W: Right. I think spring will come soon.

(W: 對。我想春天快來了。)

M: I agree.

(M: 我同意。)

Question: What season is it now?

(問題：現在是甚麼季節？)

(A)Spring.（春季。）

(B)Summer.（夏季。）

(C)Autumn.（秋季。）

(D)Winter.（冬季。）

答案：(D)

Ⅳ、Listen to the passage and decide whether the following statements are True (T) or False (F).（判斷下列句子內容是否符合你所聽到的短文內容，符合的用"T" 表示，不符合的用"F" 表示。）(6分)

Animals have homes, too.

（動物也有家。）

Everybody has a home.

（每個人有個家。）

We people have homes.

（我們人類有家。）

Animals have homes, too.

（動物也有家。）

Some animals live under the ground.

（有些動物住在地底下。）

The woodchuck lives in holes under the ground.

（土撥鼠住在地底洞穴。）

His home has two doors.

（他的家有兩個們。）

If anybody comes in one door, he goes out from the other door.
（如果任何一隻動物從一個門進來，他就會從另一個門出去）

Some birds live in nests in trees.
（有些鳥住在樹上的鳥巢裡。）

They come out for food in the daytime and go back to sleep at night.
（他們在白天出外覓食，晚上回去睡覺。）

But many birds live just in the trees.
（但是許多鳥就只是住在樹上。）

It's quite interesting that turtles carry their homes on their backs.
（很有趣的是，烏龜把他們的家帶在他們的背上。）

Bees work hard to make their homes.
（蜜蜂忙碌地建造他們的家。）

There are many, many little rooms in their house.
（在他們的房子裡有很多很多小房間。）

Cats, dogs, and chicks live in people's homes.
（貓、狗和雞住在人類的家裡。）

We see all kinds of animals in the zoo.
（我們在動物園看到各種動物。）

It is a big home for lots of animals.
（那是給許多動物的一個很大的家。）

19. Both people and animals have homes.
（人類和動物都有家。）
答案：(T 對)

20. The woodchuck lives in two rooms.
（土撥鼠住在兩間房間。）
答案：(F 錯)

21. All animals live on the ground.
（所有的動物都住在地上。）
答案：(F 錯)

22. Birds usually live in nests in trees.

（鳥類通常住在樹上的鳥巢裡。）

答案：（T 對）

23. Bees don't work hard to build their house.
（蜜蜂不努力蓋它們的房子。）

答案：（F 錯）

24. The zoo is no home for animals.
（動物園不是動物的家。）

答案：（F 錯）

V、Listen and complete the poem. （**根據你所聽到的內容，用適當的單詞完成下面的詩歌。每空格限填一詞。**）（6 分）

My two little pets（我的兩隻小寵物）
My two little pets（我的兩隻小寵物）
Are small and brown（嬌小的棕色的）
They like to jump（他們喜歡跳）
Up and down.（跳上又跳下）
Round and round（轉啊轉啊）
They go on their wheel（他們在輪子上）
And their favorite treat（他們最愛的禮物）
Is apple peel.（就是蘋果皮）
As I sit（當我坐下來）
And watch one play（看著一隻遊戲）
The other makes（另一隻在做）
A bed of hay.（稻草床）
Light and soft（又輕又軟）
They like their hay（他們喜歡他們的稻草）
To keep them warm（一直保持很溫暖）
From night till day.（好讓他們從早到晚）
My friends tell me（我的朋友告訴我）

They look like squirrels.（他們看起來像松鼠）
But I still really（但是我仍然好喜歡）
Like my two fluffy chipmunks.（我兩隻毛茸茸的土撥鼠）

My two little pets

My two little pets
Are small and __25__
They like to jump
Up and down.

Round and round
They go on their wheel
And their __26__ treat
Is apple peel.
As I sit
And watch one play
The other __27__
A bed of hay.

Light and soft
They like __28__ hay
To keep them warm
From night till day.

My friends tell me
They look __29__ squirrels.
But I still __30__
Like my two fluffy chipmunks.

25. 答案：brown (棕色的)

26. 答案：favorite (最喜愛的)

27. 答案：makes (製作)

28. 答案：their (他們的)

29. 答案：like (喜歡)

30. 答案：really (真的)

全新國中會考英語聽力精選(上)原文及參考答案

Unit 3

I 、Listen and choose the right picture.（**根據你所聽到的內容，選出相應的圖片**）（5 分）

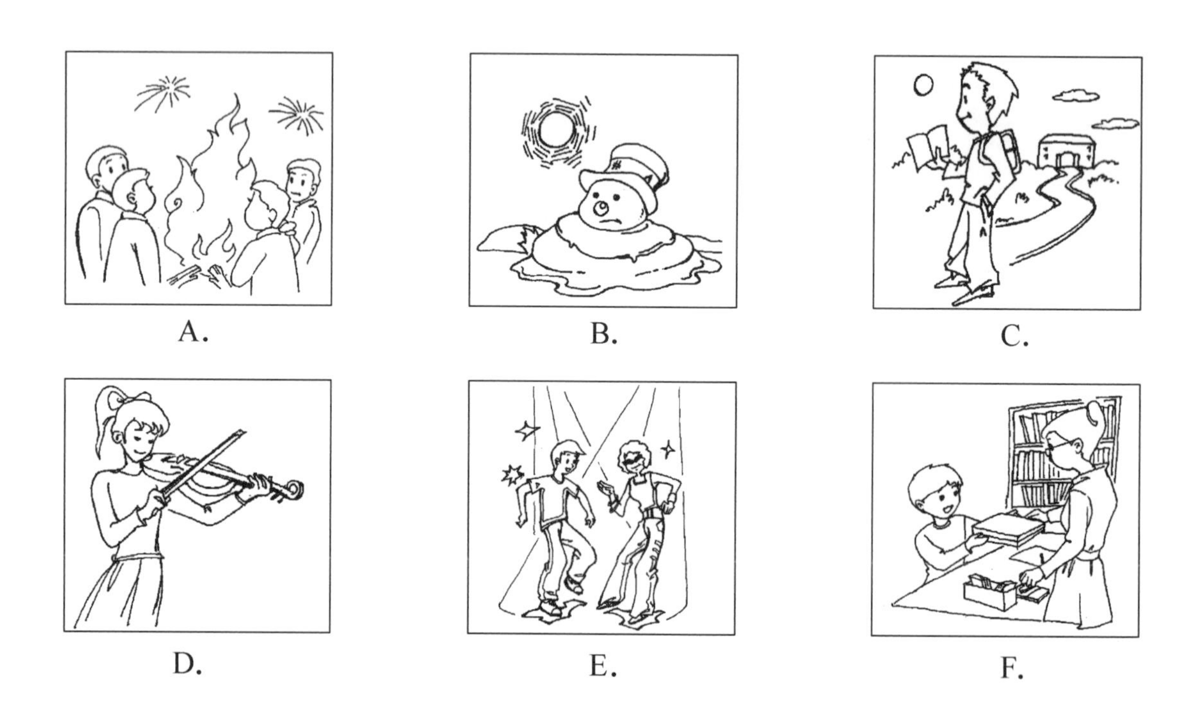

1. When winter goes by, the snowman becomes a pond of water.
   （冬天一過，雪人就變成一灘水了。）
   答案：(B)

2. Simon doesn't live far away from school so he walks to school every morning.
   （Simon 住的離學校不遠，所以他每天早上走路上學。）
   答案：(C)

3. Diana likes playing the violin very much.
   （Diana 非常喜歡拉小提琴。）
   答案：(D)

4. Today, many young people like dancing disco a lot.
   （現今，許多年輕人很喜歡跳迪斯可。）
   答案：(E)

5. Excuse me, may I borrow these books?
（不好意思，我可以借這幾本書嗎？）
答案：(F)

Ⅱ、Listen and choose the right word you hear in each sentence.（根據你所聽到的句子，選出正確的單字。）(5分)

6. Have you got a plan for the outing this weekend?
（這個周末你有了郊遊計劃嗎？）
(A)plane（飛機） (B)plan（計劃）
(C)play（遊玩） (D)pilot（駕駛）
答案：(B)

7. The trip to People's Park does not take long.
（去市民公園的這段路不會花太長時間。）
(A)sheep（羊） (B)ship（船）
(C)drop（水滴） (D)trip（旅程）
答案：(D)

8. It's a good idea to visit Spring Bay.
（去參觀 Spring 灣是個好主意。）
(A)bay（海灣） (B)buy（買）
(C)by（經由/附近的） (D)bye（再見）
答案：(A)

9. How much does the ticket to the Space Museum cost?
（太空博物館的門票要多少錢？）
(A)cast（陣容） (B)coast（海岸）
(C)cost（花費） (D)coat（外套）
答案：(C)

10. We will arrive at the museum quite soon.
（我們很快就抵達博物館了。）
(A)son（兒子） (B)soon（不久）

(C)sun（太陽）　　　　　　　　(D)so（如此）

答案：(B)

Ⅲ、Listen and choose the best response to the sentence you hear.（**根據你所聽到句子，選出最恰當的應答句。**）(5分)

11. Where have you been in Garden City?（你去過 Garden 市的哪些地方？）

(A)I have seen a lot of beautiful beaches.（我看過許多漂亮的海灘。）

(B)I live near Sandy Bay, but far away from Happy Town.
（我住在 Sandy 灣的附近，但是離 Happy 鎮很遠。）

(C)I don't live in Garden City.（我不住在 Garden 市）

(D)I have been to Space Museum in Moon Town.
（我曾去過 Moon town 的太空博物館。）

答案：(D)

12. Is Sandy Bay near or far away from Spring Bay?
（Sandy 灣離 Spring 灣近還是遠？）

(A)Yes, it's near Spring Bay.（是的，它靠近 Spring 灣。）

(B)No, it's far away from Spring Bay.（不，它離 Spring 灣很遠。）

(C)It's far away from Spring Bay.（它離 Spring 灣很遠。）

(D)It's near Sandy Bay.（它靠近 Sandy 灣。）

答案：(C)

13. Let's visit Ocean Park in Spring Bay on Saturday.
（我們周末去參觀 Spring 灣的海洋公園吧。）

(A)That's a good idea.（那是個好主意。）

(B)That's all right.（沒關係/不客氣。）

(C)Thank you.（謝謝你。）

(D)It's a good time.（這是個好時間。）

答案：(A)

14. How are we going to get there?（我們該怎麼去那裡呢？）

(A)Ten yuan.（10 元。）

(B)Let’s go by bus.（讓我們搭公車吧。）

(C)What about next Friday?（下星期五怎麼樣？）

(D)All right.（好的。）

答案：

15. What can I do for you, Mrs. White?（White 女士，我能為你做些甚麼嗎？）

(A)Thank you, Tom. Can you help me take these exercise books to your classroom?
（謝謝你，Tom。你能幫我把這些作業簿帶去你的教室嗎？）

(B)I don’t think so. You can go back to your classroom now.
（我不認為如此。你現在可以回教室了。）

(C)Can you help me, Tom?（Tom，你能幫我嗎？）

(D)That’s all right. You must do your homework now.
（沒關係。你現在必須寫功課。）

答案：(A)

Ⅳ、Listen to the dialogue and choose the best answer to the question you hear.
（根據你所聽到的對話和問題，選出最恰當的答案。）(5 分)

16. M: Where were you in the picture?（M:你這張相片是在甚麼地方？）

W: I was on the Great Wall.（W: 我在長城。）

M: Whom did you go there with?（M: 你跟誰一起去那兒的？）

W: I went there with my parents.（W: 我跟我父母去的。）

Question: Whom did the girl go to the Great Wall with?
（問題：女孩跟誰去長城？）

(A)Her sister.（她的姊妹。）

(B)Her father.（她的父親。）

(C)Her mother.（她的媽媽。）

(D)Her father and mother.（她的父親和母親。）

答案：(D)

17. W: Where did you take this photo?（W: 你在哪兒拍這張相片？）

M: I took it outside the Space Museum.（M: 我在太空博物館外面拍的。）

W: What were you doing in the photo? Were you playing a game?
（W: 你在照片裡做甚麼？你在玩遊戲嗎？）

M: No, I was talking with my friend.（M: 不，我在和我朋友說話。）

Question: What was the boy doing in the picture?（問題：照片裡的男孩在做甚麼？）

(A)He was playing a game with his friend.（他在和他的朋友玩遊戲。）

(B)He was talking to his friend.（他在和他的朋友說話。）

(C)He was playing a game with his cousin.（他在和他的表哥玩遊戲。）

(D)He was talking with his cousin.（他在和他的表哥說話。）

答案：(B)

18. W: What time are we going to get to the Ocean Park?
（W: 我們甚麼時候去海洋公園？）

M: What about nine o'clock in the morning?（M: 早上九點如何？）

W: It's too early, I think. Can we make it two hours later?
（W: 我覺得太早了。我們晚兩個小時去好嗎？）

M: Sure.（M: 當然好。）

Question: What time will they get to the Ocean Park?
（問題：他們甚麼時候要去海洋公園？）

(A)At 7 a.m.（早上七點。）

(B)At 9 a.m.（早上九點。）

(C)At 10 a.m.（早上十點。）

(D)At 11 a.m.（早上十一點。）

答案：(D)

19. M: May I have this maths book and this English book?
（M: 我買這本數學書和這本英語書好嗎？）

W: Yes. The English book costs twenty yuan and the maths book costs fifteen yuan.（W: 好的。英語書 20 元，數學書 15 元。）

M: OK.（M: 好。）

W: Do you need this magazine? It's ten yuan only.
（W: 你需要這本雜誌嗎？只要 10 元。）

M: Sorry. I don't want it.（M: 抱歉，我不要。）

Question: How much will the man spend on these books?
（問題：那個男人在這些書上要花多少錢？）

(A)35 yuan.（35 元。）

(B)30 yuan.（30 元。）

(C)25 yuan.（25 元。）

(D)45 yuan.（45 元。）

答案：(A)

20. W: There are so many things here, Dad.（W: 老爸，這裡有好多東西。）

M: Yes. Do you want a present?（M: 對。你想要個禮物嗎？）

W: Nggg ... I need a new skirt. Shall we go there?
（W: 嗯…我需要一條新裙子。我們可以去那邊嗎？）

M: OK. Let's go.（M: 好。我們走吧。）

Question: Where are they talking?（問題：他們在哪裡談話？）

(A)In the supermarket.（在超級市場。）

(B)In the park.（在公園。）

(C)In the shopping centre.（在購物中心。）

(D)In the museum.（在博物館。）

答案：(C)

V、Listen to the passage and decide whether the following statements are True (T) or False (F).（判斷下列句子內容是否符合你所聽到的短文內容，符合的用 T 表示，不符合的用 F 表示。）（5 分）

The summer holidays are coming.（暑假快來了。）

Mike, Jane and Jim are planning their holidays.
（Mike， Jane 和 Jim 正在計劃他們的假期。）

Mike would like to visit museums and go to the cinema.
（Mike 想去參觀博物館和看電影。）

He likes reading very much.（他非常喜歡看書。）

He wants to read some science fiction.（他想看一些科幻小說。）

He will go to Beijing with his parents.（他要跟他父母去北京。）

They will visit some interesting places.（他們將參觀一些有趣的地方。）

Jane likes to watch TV, so she is going to watch the long TV series.
（Jane 喜歡看電視，所以她將會看長篇電視劇。）

She would like to read some detective stories at home.（她想在家看一些偵探小說。）

She wants to go to Nanjing for a visit.（她想去南京看看。）

What about Jim?（那 Jim 呢？）

Jim will pack his books and clothes.（Jim 要打包他的書和衣服。）

His family will move into a new flat.（他的家將搬進新的公寓。）

He likes Shanghai Students' Post.（他喜歡上海學生郵報。）

He thinks it is helpful to his study.（他認為這對他的學習有幫助。）

He will go to the big supermarket near his new housing estate.
（他將會去他新家附近的超級市場。）

21. Mike, Jane and Jim are planning some activities for their winter holidays.
（Mike，Jane 和 Jim 正在為他們的寒假安排一些活動。）
答案：(F 錯)

22. Mike's parents live in Beijing and he would like to see them there.
（Mike 的父母住在北京，他想去那裡看看他們。）
答案：(F 錯)

23. Jane would like to read some science fiction during the holidays.
（Jane 想在假期中讀一些科幻小說。）
答案：(F 錯)

24. Jim won't live in their old flat and he will move into a new one.
（Jim 不住他們的老舊公寓，他將搬進一棟新的。）
答案：(T 對)

25. Jim thinks that Shanghai Students' Post is helpful to his study.
（Jim 覺得上海學生郵報對他的功課很有幫助。）
答案：(T 對)

VI、Listen to the dialogue and choose the activities Ally will do today, tomorrow and the day after tomorrow.（**根據你所聽到的對話內容，為 Ally 選出她今天、**

明天及後天將要做的事情。)(5分)

M: Hi, Ally! (M: 嗨，Ally！)

W: Hi, Andy! (W: 嗨，Andy！)

M: Ally, will you play badminton with me? (M: Ally，你要跟我去打羽毛球嗎？)

W: When? (W: 甚麼時候？)

M: This afternoon, OK? (M: 今天下午，好嗎？)

W: Sorry, I can't. I have to go to the doctor's and then study for my English test.
(W: 不好意思，我不能去。我要去看醫生，還要為我的英文測驗念書。)

M: How about tomorrow afternoon? (M: 明天下午怎麼樣？)

W: Sorry, tomorrow afternoon I will have a basketball match with my cousins and after that I will take a piano lesson.
(W: 抱歉，明天下午我和我表兄弟們有一場籃球比賽，在那之後我有鋼琴課。)

M: Well, what are you going to do the day after tomorrow? Will you be free?
(M: 好吧。後天你要做甚麼呢？你有空嗎？)

W: No, I have to look after my baby sister and cook for my grandparents.
(W: 我沒空。我要照顧我的小妹妹還要替我祖父母煮飯。)

M: Oh, I see. (M: 喔，我知道了。)

W: I'm so sorry, Andy. But I'm really very busy this week.
(W: 真抱歉，Andy。我這個星期真的很忙。)

M: Never mind. We can play badminton next week.
(M: 別介意。我們可以下星期打羽毛球。)

Things Ally will do today	Things Ally will do tomorrow	Things Ally will do the day after tomorrow
__26__	__27__ __28__	__29__ __30__

- Things Ally will do today : __26__
(Ally 今天要做的事情是：)

- Things Ally will do tomorrow：__27__、__28__
（Ally 明天要做的事情是：）
- Things Ally will do the day after tomorrow：__29__、__30__
（Ally 後天要做的事情是：）

Activities（行為）

(A) cook for her grandparents（為她的祖父母煮飯）

(B)study for a test（為一個測驗努力念書）

(C)go to the doctor's（去看醫生）

(D)take a piano lesson（上鋼琴課）

(E) have a basketball match（有一場籃球比賽）

(F) look after her baby sister（照顧她的小妹妹）

26. 答案：B
27. 答案：E
28. 答案：D
29. 答案：F
30. 答案：A

全新國中會考英語聽力精選(上)原文及參考答案

Unit 4

I、Listen and choose the right picture.(**根據你所聽到的內容，選出相應的圖片。**)
(6分)

A. B. C. D. E. F. G.

1. My neighbor Susan works as a secretary in an office in the city centre.
(我的鄰居 Susan 在市中心的一間辦公室擔任秘書的工作。)
答案：(A)

2. Would you like to be a policewoman in the future, Alice?
(Alice，你未來想當警察嗎？)
答案：(E)

3. Scientists often do experiments to find out unknown things in labs.
(科學家為了找出未知的事物經常在實驗室做實驗。)
答案：(B)

4. Who usually draws plans for tall buildings?
(通常是誰為高樓畫計劃圖？)
答案：(D)

5. Ted's father works in a famous restaurant. He is a cook.
（Ted 的父親在一家知名餐廳工作。他是一位廚師。）
答案：(C)

6. Lucy, do you want to be a doctor in the future?
（Lucy，未來你想當醫生嗎？）
答案：(G)

Ⅱ、Listen and choose the best response to the sentence you hear.（根據你所聽到的句子，選出最恰當的應答句。）（6 分）

7. What does an architect usually do?
（建築師通常做甚麼？）
(A)He draws pictures of different places.
（他畫不同地點的圖像。）
(B)He draws plans of tall buildings.
（他畫高樓的計劃圖。）
(C)He keeps our city safe and catches thieves.
（他保持城市的安全和抓小偷。）
(D)He makes sick people better and looks after them.
（他讓生病的人轉好也照顧他們。）
答案：(B)

8. Where do you work?
（你在哪裡工作？）
(A)In an office in the city centre.（在市中心的辦公室）
(B)By underground.（搭地下鐵。）
(C)At eight in the morning.（早上八點鐘。）
(D)I have no interest about it.（我對它沒興趣。）
答案：(A)

9. How is your job?
（你的工作如何？）
(A)I have been a secretary for two years.

（我當秘書有兩年了。）

(B)I go to work on foot every day.
（我每天走路上學。）

(C)I take notes and answer phones every day.
（我每天記筆記和回應電話。）

(D)I think it's interesting and I get on well with the people in my office.
（我覺得很有趣，我和辦公室裡的人相處得很好。）

答案：(D)

10. What happened to Tom yesterday?
（Tom 昨天怎麼了？）

(A)He had an accident.（他出車禍了。）

(B)He went to school.（他去學校。）

(C)He will move to a new flat.（他要搬去一個新房子。）

(D)He goes there by car.（他搭車去那兒。）

答案：(A)

11. What do you usually see on your way to school?
（在你上學的途中，你常看到甚麼？）

(A)I see many people buying newspapers from newspaper sellers.
（我看到許多人在報攤買報紙。）

(B)I usually meet my teacher on the way.
（我常常在路上遇到我老師。）

(C)I have some coffee and bread on the way to school.
（我在上學途中喝咖啡吃麵包。）

(D)I don't want to see anything on the way.
（我在路上不想看任何東西。）

答案：(A)

12. Who stopped the traffic to let the fire engine come quickly to the scene?
（誰阻擋車流好讓消防車快速抵達現場？）

(A)The doctor and the nurse.（醫生和護士。）

(B)The policeman.（警察。）

(C)The ambulance man.（消防人員。）

(D)The SPCA officer.（SPCA 官員。）

答案：(B)

Ⅲ、Listen to the dialogue and choose the best answer to the question you hear.
（根據你所聽到的對話和問題，選出最恰當的答案。）(6 分)

13. W: How many languages can you speak?
（W: 你會說幾種語言？）
M: Two. One is English and the other is German.
（M: 兩種。一種是英語，另一種是德語。）
Question: What language can the man speak?
（問題：那個男人會說甚麼語言？）
(A)English and French.（英語和法語。）
(B)English and German.（英語和德語。）
(C)English and Chinese.（英語和中文。）
(D)English.（英語。）
答案：(B)

14. M: How do you like the dishes?
（M: 這些菜你覺得如何？）
W: Delicious. Perhaps we'll come again next week.
（W: 非常好吃。或許我們下星期可以再來。）
Question: Where does the dialogue probably take place?
（問題：這段對話可能發生在哪裡？）
(A)At school.（學校。）
(B)At home.（家裡。）
(C)In a restaurant.（餐廳。）
(D)In the hospital.（醫院。）
答案：(C)

15. M: Don't call out, Linda. Your mother is sleeping in the next room.
（M: Linda，不要喊叫。你母親在隔壁房間睡覺。）
W: But there's a telephone call for her.

（W: 但是有她的電話。）

Question: What does Linda want her mother to do?

（問題：Linda 想要她母親做甚麼？）

(A)She wants her to go to bed early.

（她想讓她母親早點睡。）

(B)She wants her to go shopping with them.

（她想讓她跟她們一起去逛街。）

(C)She wants her not to make any noise.

（她想要她不要發出噪音。）

(D)She wants her to answer a phone call.

（她想讓她接電話。）

答案：(D)

16. M: Would you like to go to the cinema with me tonight?

（M: 你今晚要跟我一起去電影院嗎？）

W: Sorry, I'm too tired. But thank you all the same.

（W: 抱歉。我很累。但一樣謝謝你。）

Question: Why isn't she going to the cinema?

（問題：為什麼她不去電影院？）

(A)She's too busy.（她太忙了。）

(B)She is seeing a film.（她在看影片。）

(C)She's too tired.（她太累了。）

(D)She has something to do.（她沒事可做。）

答案：(C)

17. M: I want to work during the summer holidays.

（M: 我想在暑假工作。）

W: What kind of work would you like to do?

（W: 你想做甚麼種類的工作？）

M: Any kind. I just want to get some working experiences.

（M:任何種類。我就是想要有一些工作經驗。）

Question: What is the boy going to do during the summer holidays?

（問題：這個男孩在暑假要做甚麼？）

(A)He's going to work to get some working experiences.
（他要工作來得到一些工作經驗。）

(B)He's going to travel by air.
（他將搭飛機旅行。）

(C)He has found a good job.
（他已經找到一份很好的工作。）

(D)He has got many experiences.
（他已經有很多經驗。）

答案：(A)

18. W: Where's Jenny?
（W: Jenny 在哪裡？）

M: I don't know. Maybe she's in the teachers' office now. What do you want her for?
（M: 我不知道。或許她現在在老師辦公室。你找她做甚麼？）

W: I want to borrow her bicycle.
（W: 我想向她借腳踏車。）

Question: Where is Jenny probably?
（問題：Jenny 可能在哪裡？）

(A)In her home.（在她家。）

(B)In the teachers' office.（在老師辦公室。）

(C)On the playground.（在遊戲場。）

(D)On her bike.（在她的腳踏車上。）

答案：(B)

Ⅳ、Listen to the passage and decide whether the following statements are True (T) or False (F).（判斷下列句子內容是否符合你所聽到的短文內容，符合的用"T" 表示，不符合的用"F" 表示。）（6 分）

Susan is at the cinema.
（Susan 在電影院。）

She is enjoying the film very much.
（她非常喜歡這部電影。）

A man sits next to her.
（一個男人坐在她旁邊。）

He is looking for something.
（他在找東西。）

Susan gets angry.
（Susan 很生氣。）

She says to him in a low voice, "What are you looking for?"
（她小聲的對他說：「你在找甚麼？」）

"A piece of chocolate!" the man says. "It's on the floor."
（「一片巧克力！」那個男人說，「它在地上。」）

"A piece of chocolate?" Susan is surprised.
（「一片巧克力？」Susan 很訝異。）

She says angrily, "It will be dirty now! Take this piece and sit still, please. I can't watch the film!"
（她生氣地說：「它現在一定很髒了。拿著這片，然後請坐著不要動。我沒辦法看電影！」）

Then she gives the man a piece of chocolate.
（然後她給了那個男人一片巧克力。）

"I can't eat this. My teeth are on the piece of chocolate on the floor!" answers the man.
（「我不能吃這個。我的牙齒在地上的那片巧克力上面。」男人回答。）

19. Susan likes the film very much.
（Susan 非常喜歡那部電影。）
答案：（T 對）

20. Susan knows the man next to her.
（Susan 認識她隔壁的那個男人。）
答案：（F 錯）

21. The man is looking for the chocolate, because it's Susan's.
（那個男人在找巧克力，因為巧克力是 Susan 的。）
答案：（F 錯）

22. Susan gets angry, because she can't watch the film.

（Susan 很生氣，因為她不能看電影。）

答案：(T 對)

23. The man doesn't want to find the chocolate on the floor.

（那個男人不想找地上的巧克力。）

答案：(F 錯)

24. In fact, the man is looking for his teeth.

（事實上，那個男人在找他的牙齒。）

答案：(T 對)

V、Listen and fill in the blanks.（**根據你所聽到的內容，用適當的單詞完成下面的句子。每空格限填一詞。**）(6 分)

My cousin Peter was ten.

（我表弟 Peter 十歲。）

He was interested in reading.

（他對閱讀很感興趣。）

He studied in a school near his home.

（他就讀他家附近的一所學校。）

But he had no money.

（但是他沒有錢。）

His family was very poor.

（他家非常窮。）

He could not buy any books.

（他買不了任何書。）

One day he had a good idea.

（有一天他有一個好點子。）

He thought he would like to find a job and then he could get some money to buy books.

（他想，他想去找一份工作然後他就有錢買書。）

A week later he got his first job.

（一周後他找到他第一份工作。）

That was to send newspapers to many houses.
（是到很多家送報紙。）

The boss told him, “You will get three dollars an hour, and next year you will make five dollars an hour.”
（老闆對他說：「你一小時可以得到三塊錢，明年你每小時就有五塊錢。」）

“That’s wonderful!” Peter said, “I will see you next year.”
（「太棒了！」Peter 說，「明年再見。」）

- Peter was __25__ years old.
  （Peter ____歲。）
- Peter was interested in __26__.
  （Peter 對____很感興趣。）
- Peter thought he would like to find a job and then he could __27__ some money to buy books.
  （Peter 想，他想找一份工作然後他就____一些錢來買書。）
- Peter’s first job was to send __28__ to many houses.
  （Peter 的第一份工作是去許多人家送____。）
- The boss told Peter that the next year he would make __29__ dollars an hour.
  （老闆告訴 Peter 明年他每小時可以賺____塊錢。）
- Peter said to the boss, “I will see you __30__ year.”
  （Peter 對老闆說：「____再見！」）

25. 答案：10/ten (十)

26. 答案：reading (閱讀)

27. 答案：get (得到)

28. 答案：newspapers (報紙)

29. 答案：5/five (五)

30. 答案：Next (下一個)

全新國中會考英語聽力精選(上)原文及參考答案

Unit 5

I、Listen and choose the right picture.(根據你所聽到的內容，選出相應的圖片。)(6分)

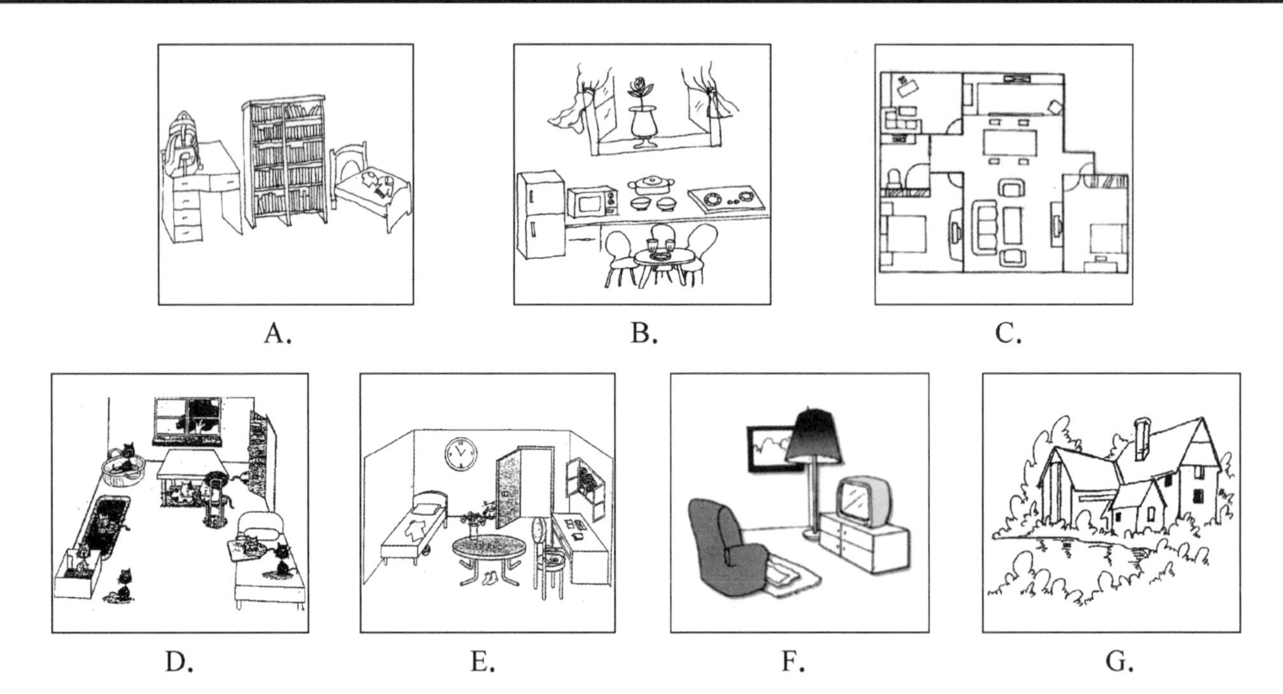

A. B. C. D. E. F. G.

1. The kitchen is my mother's favorite in our flat. She enjoys cooking very much.
(我們家裡我母親最喜歡的就是廚房。他非常喜歡煮菜。)
答案：(B)

2. Take a look at the blue-print picture. I think we need a flat with two bedrooms and two bathrooms.
(看一下這張藍圖。我想我們需要一間兩房兩衛的公寓。)
答案：(C)

3. Shall I put on some more decorations in my bedroom? Now, it looks nice and tidy.
(我在我的臥室放多一點裝飾品好嗎？現在它看起來不錯也很整齊。)
答案：(E)

4. Sam, go to the study. It's time for you to do your homework.
(Sam，去念書。現在是你做功課的時間了。)
答案：(A)

5. On Sunday afternoons, I often sit in the sofa, enjoying my favorite TV plays in the sitting room.
（在星期天下午，我常坐在客廳的沙發上欣賞我最喜歡的電視劇。）
答案：(F)

6. The Smiths live in a big house in the suburbs.
（Smith 一家人住在郊外的大房子裡。）
答案：(G)

Ⅱ、Listen and choose the best response to the sentence you hear.（根據你所聽到的句子，選出最恰當的應答句。）（6 分）

7. Oh, Ben! Your room looks quite dirty.
（喔，Ben！你的房間看起來真髒。）
(A)Never mind.（別介意。）
(B)Thank you.（謝謝你。）
(C)It's OK.（沒關係。）
(D)Sorry. I'll clean it now.（抱歉。我現在來清掃。）
答案：(D)

8. Sir, what can I do for you?
（先生，我能為你服務嗎？）
(A)I want to look for a bigger flat for my family.
（我想為我家人找一間大房子。）
(B)Your office looks very nice.
（你的辦公室看起來很不錯。）
(C)Thank you for your help.
（謝謝你的幫忙。）
(D)That's all right. Welcome again.
（沒關係。歡迎再來。）
答案：(A)

9. What kind of flat would you like?
（你喜歡怎樣的公寓？）

(A)I live in a flat with three bedrooms and two sitting rooms.
（我住在三房兩廳的公寓。）

(B)Betty wants a flat with three bedrooms and a big balcony.
（Betty 想要有三個房間、一個大陽台的公寓。）

(C)You can do some exercise every morning on the balcony, I think.
（我想你可以每天早上在陽台做運動。）

(D)I'm looking for a flat with two bedrooms, one kitchen and two bathrooms.
（我在找一間兩房、兩衛、一間廚房的公寓。）

答案：(D)

10. How much shall we pay for the flat each month?
（我們每個月要為這間房子付多少錢？）

(A)It's ￥1,800,000 altogether.（一共一百八十萬元。）

(B)Is ￥2,500 enough?（兩千五百元夠嗎？）

(C)It's ￥2,700 a month.（一個月兩千七百元。）

(D)￥25,000 a year. OK?（一年兩萬五千元好嗎？）

答案：(C)

11. How is your flat in Happy Estate, Judy?
（Judy，妳在 Happy Estate 的房子怎麼樣？）

(A)I like it very much.（我非常喜歡它。）

(B)I don't like it at all.（我一點也不喜歡它。）

(C)It's much bigger than the old one.（它比舊的那個大。）

(D)The old one is much better.（舊的那個好多了。）

答案：(C)

12. Is it convenient for you to travel to school from your new flat?
（從你新家到學校的交通方便嗎？）

(A)Yes, it is.（是的，很方便。）

(B)No, it wasn't.（不，不方便。）

(C)Yes, I did.（是的，我做了。）

(D)No, I won't.（不，我不要。）

答案：(A)

Ⅲ、Listen to the dialogue and choose the best answer to the question you hear.
（根據你所聽到的對話和問題，選出最恰當的答案。）（6 分）

13. M: Would you hurry up? The play starts at 7.30.
（M: 你可以快一點嗎？表演七點半就開始了。）

W: Don't worry. We still have 20 minutes.
（W: 別擔心。我們還有二十分鐘。）

Question: What time is it now?
（問題：現在幾點？）

(A)7.10.（七點十分。）

(B)7.20.（七點二十分。）

(C)7.30.（七點三十分。）

(D)7.50.（七點五十分。）

答案：(A)

14. M: Mary, have you seen my older brother, Billy? I can't find him anywhere.
（M: Mary, 你看到我哥哥 Billy 了嗎？我到處找不到他。）

W: I saw him leaving with Peter and Dick a few minutes ago.
（W: 幾分鐘以前我看到他與 Peter、Dick 一起離開。）

Question: Who is the man looking for?
（問題：那個男人在找誰？）

(A)Mary.（Mary。）

(B)Peter.（Peter。）

(C)Dick.（Dick。）

(D)Billy.（Billy。）

答案：(D)

15. M: What's the matter with Billy?
（M: Billy 怎麼了？）

W: He fell off the bicycle near the shopping centre on his way to school. He has been taken to the hospital.
（W: 他在上學途中，靠近購物中心的附近從腳踏車上摔下來。他已經被送去醫院了。）

M: Oh, I hope there is nothing serious.
(M: 喔。我希望不會太嚴重。)

W: I hope not.
(W: 我也希望。)

Question: Where is Billy now?
(問題：Billy 現在在哪裡？)

(A)At home.(在家。)

(B)In the school.(在學校。)

(C)In the hospital.(在醫院。)

(D)Near the shopping centre.(靠近購物中心。)

答案：(C)

16. M: What does your father do, Betty?
(M: Betty，你父親做甚麼的？)

W: He used to be a worker, but now he is an engineer.
(W: 他以前是一位工人，但是他現在是工程師。)

M: What do you want to be when you grow up?
(M: 當你長大的時候，你想當甚麼？)

W: I want to be a doctor. I don't want to be a nurse like my mother.
(W: 我想當醫生。我不想像我母親一樣當護士。)

Question: What does Betty's mother do?
(問題：Betty 的母親做甚麼？)

(A)A worker.(職工。)

(B)A doctor.(醫生。)

(C)A nurse.(護士。)

(D)An engineer.(工程師。)

答案：(C)

17. M: Are you going to the flower show this afternoon, Mary?
(M: Mary，今天下午你要去花卉展覽嗎？)

W: I hope I can, but I have a lot of homework to do.
(W: 我希望我可以，但是我有好多功課要做。)

M: What about John?

(M: John 呢？)

W: He is going to stay at home and watch a football match on TV.

(W: 他要待在家在電視上看足球賽。)

M: What a shame!

(M: 真可惜！)

Question: What is Mary going to do this afternoon?

(問題：Mary 今天下午要做甚麼？)

(A)To do a lot of homework.(做很多功課。)

(B)To go to the flower show.(去花卉展覽。)

(C)To watch a football match.(看足球賽。)

(D)To watch TV.(看電視。)

答案：(A)

18. M: How did you like yesterday's performances?

(M: 你覺得昨天的表演如何？)

W: I enjoyed them very much.

(W: 我非常享受。)

M: Which item did you like best?

(M: 你最喜歡哪一個項目？)

W: I liked the short play best.

(W: 我最喜歡那個短劇。)

M: So did I. I thought the cross talk was better than the recitation and the group singing.

(M：我也是。我覺得相聲比朗誦和團體演唱來得好。)

W: I thought so, too.

(W: 我也這麼認為。)

Question: Which item did they like best?

(問題：他們最喜歡哪個項目？)

(A)The cross talk.(相聲。)

(B)The short play.(短劇。)

(C)The group singing.(團體演唱。)

(D)The recitation.(朗誦。)

答案：(B)

Ⅳ、Listen to the passage and decide whether the following statements are True (T) or False (F). (判斷下列句子內容是否符合你所聽到的短文內容，符合的用"T" 表示，不符合的用"F" 表示。)(6分)

It is Sunday today.
(今天星期天。)

The Li's are going to move into a new flat, so Mr. Li calls the removal company for help.
(Li 家要搬進新房子，因此 Li 先生叫了搬家公司來幫忙。)

At the same time, Mrs. Li is putting things into big suitcases.
(在此同時，Li 太太把東西放進行李箱裡。)

Li Hua is helping her mother.
(Li Hua 幫他母親。)

Her brother, Li Ming is playing on the computer.
(他弟弟 Li Ming 在玩電腦。)

Half an hour later, three removal men arrive.
(半小時候，三個搬家工人來了。)

They put many heavy things and Li Ming's computer onto a truck and drive away to the Li's new flat.
(他們把很多很重的東西和 Li Ming 的電腦搬上卡車，駛向 Li 家的新家。)

Mr. Li drives his own car and carries the big suitcases.
(Li 先生開他自己的車，帶了很多行李。)

They are all happy.
(他們都非常開心。)

The flat is in the suburbs and it's bigger than the old one.
(房子在郊區而且比舊的大。)

Li Hua and Li Ming can have their own bedrooms.
(Li Hua 和 Li Ming 可以有他們自己的房間。)

Although it's not very convenient for the children to go to school, it's a quiet and beautiful place.
（雖然對孩子來說上學不是很方便，但是那是一個安靜又美麗的地方。）

They can go to the city center in Mr. Li's car.
（他們可以坐 Li 先生的車去市中心。）

And there will be an underground station by the end of the year.
（而年底將有地鐵車站。）

19. The Li's are going to help others move into a new flat.
（Li 家將幫其他人搬進新房子。）
答案：(F 錯)

20. Li Ming is helping his mother with the suitcases.
（Li Ming 幫助他母親處理行李。）
答案：(F 錯)

21. There are at least three bedrooms in the new flat.
（新房子至少有三個房間。）
答案：(T 對)

22. The new flat is near Li Hua's school.
（新房子離 Li Hua 的學校很近。）
答案：(F 錯)

23. They can go to other places by car or by underground next year.
（他們可以搭車去其他地方，明年可以搭地鐵。）
答案：(T 對)

24. Their new flat is in a quiet and beautiful place.
（他們的新房子在一個安靜又美麗的地方。）
答案：(T 對)

V、Listen to the dialogue and complete the plan.（**根據你所聽到的對話內容，用適當的單詞完成下面的平面圖。**）(6 分)

Danny and Susan are talking about Susan's new flat.
（Danny 和 Susan 在談論 Susan 的新房子）

M: I hear that you have moved into a new flat, Susan.
（M: Susan，我聽說你搬到新房子了。）

W: Yes, it's bigger than my old flat. It's near my school. There are two bedrooms, a living room, a bathroom and a kitchen in it.
（W: 是的。它比我的舊房子大。它離我學校很近。它有兩個房間、一個客廳、一間浴室和一間廚房。）

M: You can have your own room now.
（M: 你現在可以有自己的房間了。）

W: Yes, I study and sleep in the smaller bedroom. There is a bookshelf next to the door. My bed is in the front of the room, so I can have fresh air every day.
（W: 是的。我在比較小的房間裡念書和睡覺。門的旁邊有一個書架。我的床在房間的前面，所以我每天都會有新鮮空氣。）

M: Do your parents sleep in another room?
（M: 你父母睡另一個房間嗎？）

W: Yes. And they put a colorful wardrobe on the left of their room.
（W: 是的。他們在他們房間的左邊放了一個彩色的衣櫃。）

M: Are there any balconies?
（M: 有陽台嗎？）

W: Yes, but there is only one. It's in my parents' room, opposite the door.
（W: 有，但是只有一個。在我父母的房間，門的對面。）

M: What do you think about the living room?
（M: 你覺得客廳怎麼樣？）

W: It's quite big! We put a rug in front of the entrance.
（W: 很大！我們在入口前放了一個地毯。）

M: Do you have dinner in the living room?
（M: 你們在客廳吃晚餐嗎？）

W: Yes, we put the table beside the kitchen. We bought a new TV set and put it in the middle of the living room. The sofa is opposite the TV set. The armchair is near the sofa, so my father sometimes has a rest in the armchair after dinner.
（W: 是，我們在廚房旁邊放了餐桌。我們買了一台新電視，放在客廳的中間。沙發在電視機的對面，所以我爸爸有時候會在晚餐後在扶手椅上休息。）

M: Have you bought a new fridge in your kitchen?

（M: 你們的廚房裡買了新冰箱嗎？）

W: No, but we are going to buy one this weekend. There's only a cupboard in the kitchen now.

（W: 沒買。但是我們將在這個周末去買一台。現在廚房只有一個碗櫃。）

M: Well, enjoy every day in your new flat.

（M: 希望在你的新房子享受每一天。）

W: Thank you! And welcome to my new flat next time.

（W: 謝謝你。下次歡迎來我的新房子。）

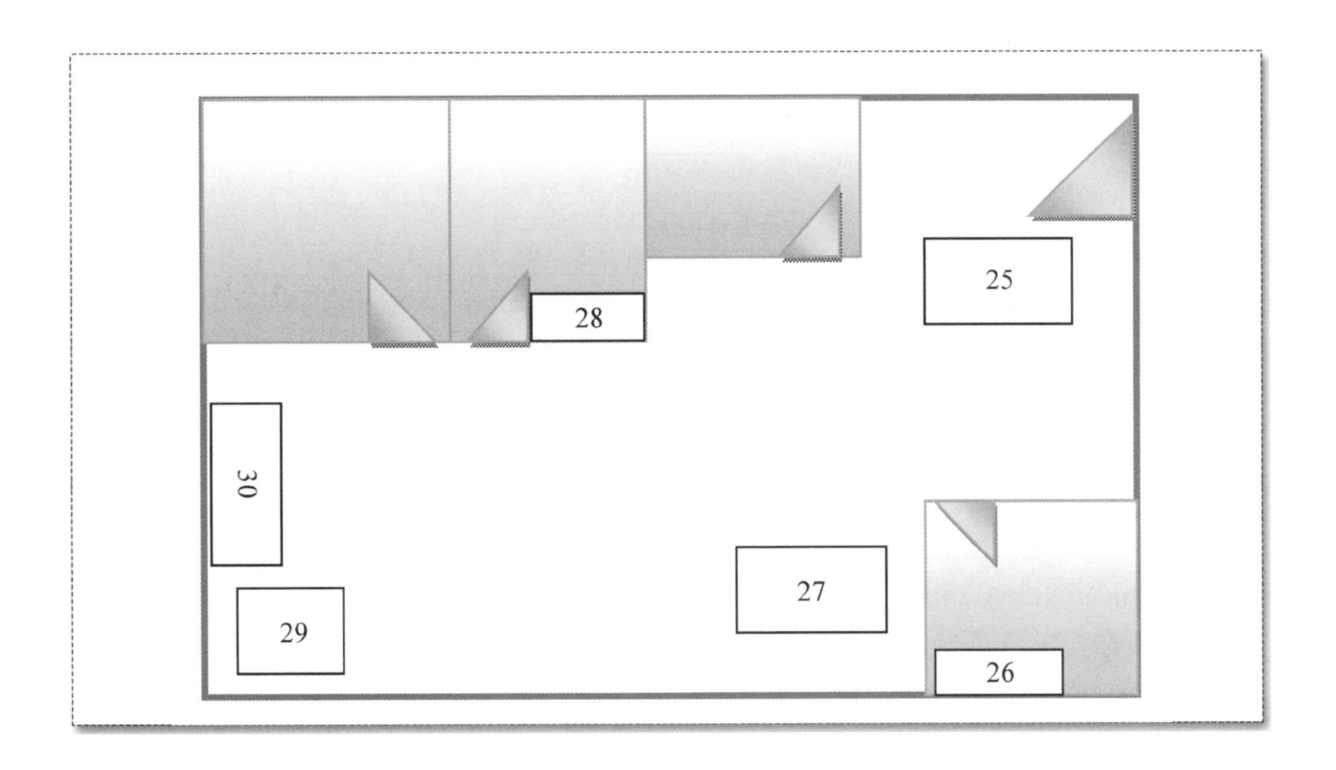

25. 答案：rug (地毯)
26. 答案：cupboard (碗櫃)
27. 答案：(dinner) table ((晚餐)餐桌)
28. 答案：bookshelf (書櫃)
29. 答案：armchair (扶手椅)
30. 答案：sofa (沙發)

全新國中會考英語聽力精選(上)原文及參考答案

Unit 6

I 、Listen and choose the right picture.（**根據你所聽到的內容，選出相應的圖片**）（5 分）

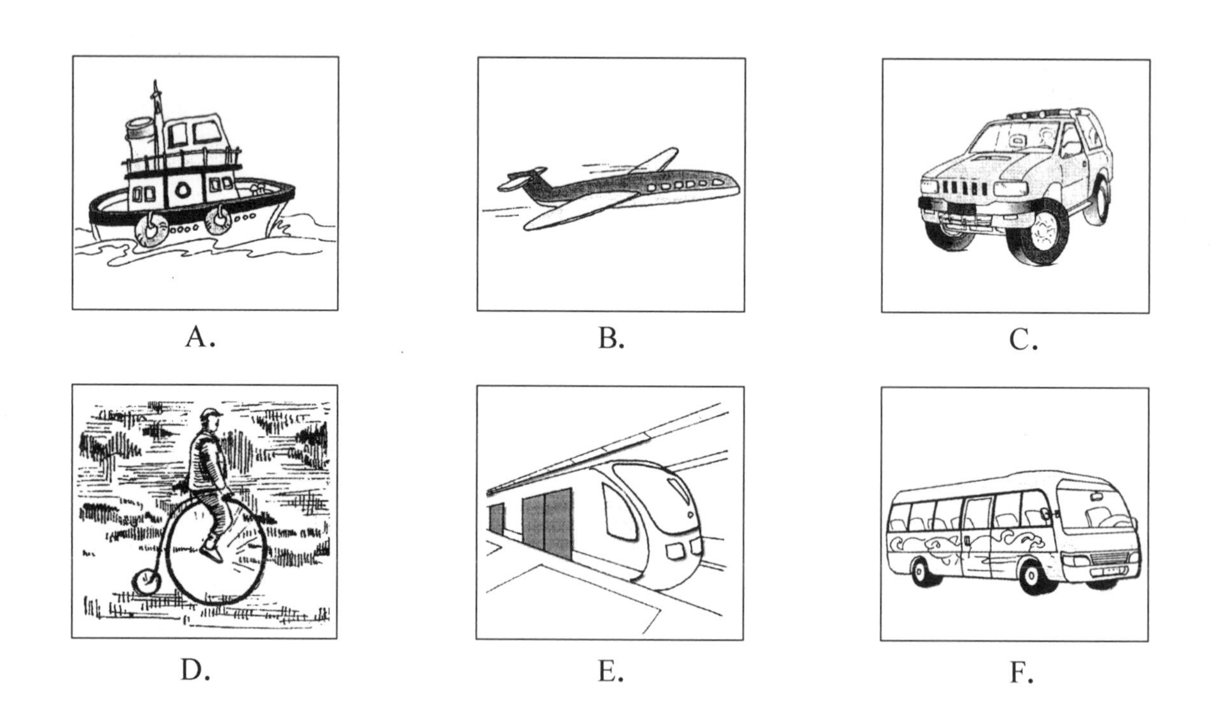

A. B. C.

D. E. F.

1. Long ago, bicycles looked quite different from the ones nowadays.
   （很久以前，腳踏車看起來和現在的相當不同。）
   答案：(D)

2. More and more people like taking the underground to work.
   （越來越多人喜歡搭地鐵去上班。）
   答案：(E)

3. Nowadays, not many people go from Puxi to Pudong by ferry.
   （現在從浦西搭乘渡輪到浦東的人不多。）
   答案：(A)

4. It's not very expensive to take the planes to different places now.
   （現在搭飛機去其他地方不是非常昂貴。）
   答案：(B)

5. There is a bus in our school. Sometimes we take it to some places.
（學校有一輛公車。有時候我們搭乘公車去一些地方。）

答案：(F)

II、Listen and choose the right word you hear in each sentence.（根據你所聽到的句子，選出正確的單字。）（5 分）

6. Read the notice on the information board.（閱讀資訊看板上的通知。）

(A)body（身體） (B)bread（麵包）
(C)board（板子） (D)boy（男孩）

答案：(C)

7. Every Sunday, Danny's family goes to church on foot.
（每個星期天，Danny 一家人走路去教堂。）

(A)children（孩子們） (B)catch（捕捉）
(C)church（教堂） (D)choir（合唱團）

答案：(C)

8. My mother read a story to me every night when I was young.
（當我小的時候，我媽媽每晚念故事給我聽。）

(A)storm（暴風雨） (B)store（商店）
(C)story（故事） (D)study（研究/學習）

答案：(C)

9. Are you ready for the football match?（足球賽你準備好了嗎？）

(A)read（閱讀） (B)ready（準備）
(C)really（真實的） (D)rainy（下雨的）

答案：(B)

10. It's only 30 minutes' walk from the city center to our school.
（從市中心到我們學校步行只要 30 分鐘。）

(A)minute（分鐘） (B)minus（減）
(C)many（許多） (D)menu（菜單）

答案：(A)

Ⅲ、Listen and choose the best response to the sentence you hear.（**根據你所聽到句子，選出最恰當的應答句。**）（5分）

11. Do you live near or far away from your school?（你住的離學校很近還是很遠？）
(A)Yes, I live near my school.（是的，我住學校附近。）
(B)No, I live far from my school.（不，我住的離學校很遠。）
(C)I live near my school.（我住學校附近。）
(D)Sorry, I don't know.（抱歉，我不知道。）
答案：(C)

12. How do you go to school every day?（你每天怎麼去學校？）
(A)About half an hour.（大約半小時。）
(B)By car.（搭車。）
(C)A long way to go.（要走很長的路。）
(D)In five minutes.（在五分鐘之內。）
答案：(B)

13. How long does it take you to get to school from your home?
（從你家到學校要花多久時間？）
(A)I see a post office.（我看到一間郵局。）
(B)By taxi.（搭計程車。）
(C)A few parents.（一些父母。）
(D)It takes about an hour.（大約一小時。）
答案：(D)

14. What do you usually see on your way to school?（你在上學的路上常看到甚麼？）
(A)I see a lot of parents and students, a few teachers and some shops.
（我看到很多父母和學生，一些老師，和一些商店。）
(B)I see some books in it.（我看到裡面有一些書。）
(C)I can't see anything on the way.（我一路上看不到任何東西。）
(D)I like walking to school and talking to my friends.
（我喜歡走路上學，跟我朋友說話。）

答案：(A)

15. When will our parents listen to the school choir?
（我們的父母何時會聽學校合唱團唱歌？）

(A)At three fifteen.（在 3 點 15 分。）

(B)In the school hall.（在學校大堂。）

(C)At the school entrance.（在學校入口。）

(D)On the second floor.（在二樓。）

答案：(A)

Ⅳ、Listen to the dialogue and choose the best answer to the question you hear.
（根據你所聽到的對話和問題，選出最恰當的答案。）(5 分)

16. M: I need to meet my cousin from the USA at the airport.
（M: 我需要在機場和我從美國來的表哥碰面。）

W: Shanghai Pudong International Airport is far away from here. You can take a taxi there.
（W: 上海浦東國際機場離這裡非常遠。你可以搭計程車去那兒。）

M:But it's too expensive. I think I can take the Maglev. It's much quicker and cheaper.
（M: 但是那太貴了。我想我可以搭磁浮列車。它快多了而且比較便宜。）

W: That's a good idea.W: 那是個好主意。）

Question: How will the man get to the airport?（問題：男人要怎麼去機場？）

(A)By car.（搭車。）

(B)By taxi.（搭計程車。）

(C)By underground. 搭地鐵。）

(D)By Maglev.（搭磁浮列車。）

答案：(D)

17. W: What can you see when you are walking to school?
（W: 你走路上學的時候你會看到甚麼？）

M: I can see a lot of students and parents, a few shops and some restaurants when I am walking to school.

（M: 我走路上學的時候，我可以看到許多學生、老師，一些商店和餐廳。）

Question: What can't the boy see on his way to school?
（問題：男孩上學的路上看不到甚麼？）

(A)Parents.（父母。）

(B)Traffic lights.（交通號誌。）

(C)Shops.（商店。）

(D)Restaurants.（餐廳。）

答案：(B)

18. M: Where are you going?（M: 你要去哪兒？）

W: I'm going to the supermarket.（W: 我要去超級市場。）

M: How long does it take you to get there?（M: 你去那裡要花多久時間？）

W: It takes about ten minutes by bus, but about half an hour on foot.
（W: 搭公車要十分鐘，但是走路大約要半小時。）

Question: How long does it take the girl to walk to the supermarket?
（問題：女孩走路去超級市場要花多久時間？）

(A)5 minutes.（五分鐘。）

(B)10 minutes.（十分鐘。）

(C)20 minutes.（二十分鐘。）

(D)30 minutes.（三十分鐘。）

答案：(D)

19. M: Tomorrow is a holiday. I'm going to the cinema with my cousin.
（M: 明天是假日。我要跟我表哥去電影院。）

W: Can I go to the cinema with you?（W: 我可以跟你一起去電影院嗎？）

M: Aren't you going to stay in bed all day?（M: 你不是要整天待在床上嗎？）

W: No. I'm going to enjoy myself tomorrow.（W: 不，我明天要享受一下。）

Question: What does the girl mean?（問題：女孩的意思是？）

(A)She wants to stay in bed all day.（她想整天待在床上。）

(B)She wants to visit the boy's home tomorrow.（她明天想拜訪那個男孩的家。）

(C)She wants to have a good time tomorrow.（她希望明天玩得開心。）

(D)She wants to have a holiday tomorrow.（她希望明天有個假期。）

答案：(C)

20. M: What are you going to do tomorrow, Jane?
（M: Jane，你明天要做甚麼？）

W: I don't know. What are you going to do, Peter?
（W: 我不知道。Peter，你要做甚麼呢？）

M: I'm going to play with my friends.（M: 我要跟我朋友去玩。）

W: Where are you going to play?（W: 你們要去哪裡玩？）

M: We're going to catch the underground to Pudong. Can you go with us?
（M: 我們要搭地鐵去浦東。你能跟我們去嗎？）

W: All right. I've got a holiday tomorrow.（W: 可以。我明天放假。）

M: Thanks, Jane.（M: Jane，謝謝。）

Question: What will Jane do tomorrow?（問題：Jane 明天要做甚麼？）

(A)She will stay at home.（她會待在家。）

(B)She will play with Peter's friends in Pudong.（她會在浦東和 Peter 的朋友玩。）

(C)She will catch the underground to People's Square.（她會在人民廣場搭地鐵。）

(D)I don't know what she will do tomorrow.（我不知道她明天要做甚麼。）

答案：(B)

V、Listen to the passage and decide whether the following statements are True (T) or False (F).（判斷下列句子內容是否符合你所聽到的短文內容，符合的用 T 表示，不符合的用 F 表示。）(5 分)

Yao Ming is a basketball player.（姚明是一位籃球員。）

But now he is a film star, too.（但是他現在也是一位電影明星。）

There is a film about Yao Ming.（有一部關於姚明的電影。）

Its name is The Year of Yao.（片名是「姚之年」。）

Americans made the film.（美國人製作這部電影。）

Now it has come to China.（現在也來到了中國。）

The film lasts for 88 minutes.（電影片長 88 分鐘。）

It is about Yao Ming's first year in the NBA.（是有關姚明在 NBA 的第一年。）

Some NBA stars talk about Yao Ming in the film.
（一些 NBA 明星在影片裡談到姚明。）

So you can see Michael Jordan and Shaquille O'Neal in it.
（所以你可以在裡面看到 Michael Jordan 和 Shaquille O' Neal。）

The film can help us know more about Yao Ming.
（這部電影可以幫助我們更認識姚明。）

Let's go to the cinema.（讓我們去電影院吧！）

21. Yao Ming plays for Huanghe Football Team.（姚明替黃河足球隊打球。）

答案：(F 錯)

22. The film was made in the USA.（這部影片是美國拍的。）

答案：(T 對)

23. The film lasts for about one and a half hours.（這部影片長度大約一個半小時。）

答案：(T 對)

24. You can see Liu Xiang in the film.（你可以在這部電影中看見劉湘。）

答案：(F 錯)

25. The film can help you know more about Yao Ming.（這部電影能幫助你更了解姚明。）

答案：(T 對)

VI、Listen to the passage and complete the notice. (**根據你所聽到的短文內容，用適當的單詞或數字完成下面的通知。每空格限填一個單詞或數字。**)(5 分)

Today is Sunday.（今天是星期天。）

Our class meets at seven thirty a.m. at the school gate.
（上午七點半我們班在學校大門口碰面。）

We take a bus to Hai'an Park.（我們搭公車去 Hai' an 公園。）

The price of the ticket for each adult is eighteen yuan, but for each student it's half.（每個成人的票價是 18 元，但是學生半價。）

The park is open from 8 a.m. to 5 p.m.（公園從上午八點開放到下午五點。）

First we play games in the park.（首先我們在公園裡玩遊戲。）
And then we have lunch at noon.（然後中午的時候吃午餐。）
After that we sit and chat under the tree.（之後我們坐在樹下聊天。）
At half past three, we go to the Swimming Club.（三點半，我們去游泳俱樂部。）
We come back home at about six o'clock in the afternoon because it is time for all of us to have dinner.（我們在下午六點回家，因為這是我們吃晚餐的時間。）
We are tired but we are very happy.（我們很累但是我們非常開心。）

Programme: （節目安排：）

- __26__ a.m.（上午____ 點）: meet at the school gate（在學校門口集合）
- Activities in the park:（公園的活動：）
  play __27__（玩）
  have __28__（吃）

sit and chat under the tree（坐在樹下聊天）
go to the Swimming__29__（去游泳 ______）

- 6 p.m.： go home（下午六點：回家）

Other information:（其他訊息：）
Ticket price: ¥__30__/child（票價：______元/孩童）

26. 答案：7.30/seven thirty/half past seven（七點半）
27. 答案：games（遊戲）
28. 答案：lunch（午餐）
29. 答案：Club（俱樂部）
30. 答案：9/nine（九）

全新國中會考英語聽力精選(上)原文及參考答案

Unit 7

I、Listen and choose the right picture.（根據你所聽到的內容,選出相應的圖片。）（6分）

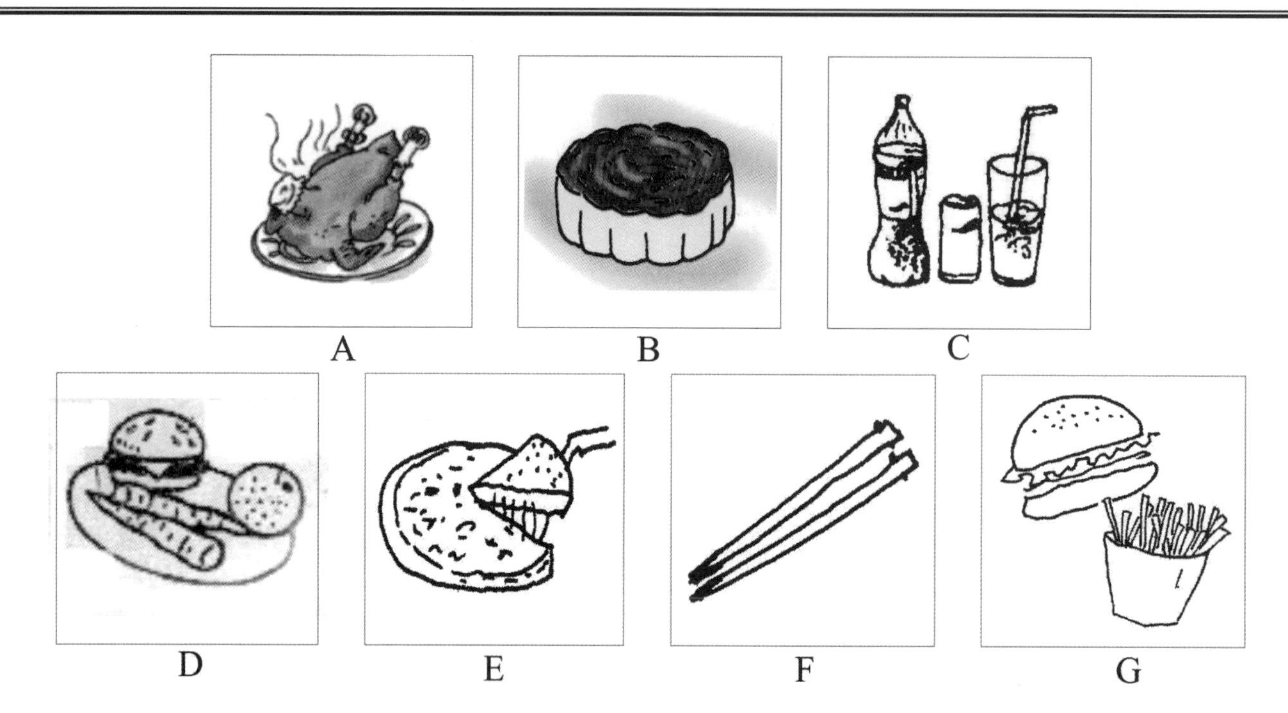

1. Western people eat turkey on Thanksgiving Day.
（西方人在感恩節的時候吃火雞。）
答案：(A)

2. Our English teacher has taught us how to make some icy drinks by ourselves.
（我們英文老師教過我們該怎麼自己做一些冰的飲料。）
答案：(C)

3. David is used to eating Chinese food with chopsticks.
（David 習慣用筷子吃中國食物。）
答案：(F)

4. The Mid-autumn Festival is coming. My dad has bought some mooncakes.
（中秋節快到了。我爸爸買了一些月餅。）
答案：(B)

5. I'm going to buy some Italian food, for example, pizza.
（我要去買一些意大利食物，比如比薩。）
答案：(E)

6. Let's go to the McDonald's to have some hamburgers and French fries.
（我們去麥當勞吃漢堡和薯條吧。）
答案：(G)

II、Listen and choose the best response to the sentence you hear.（**根據你所聽到的句子,選出最恰當的應答句。**）(6 分)

7. What about having a drink?（喝點東西怎麼樣？）
(A)That sounds great.（聽起來不錯。）
(B)I don't like any drinks.（我不喜歡任何飲料。）
(C)Let's have some drinks.（我們來喝點東西吧。）
(D)Drinks are good for us.（飲料對我們有好處。）
答案：(A)

8. What is the weather like today?（今天天氣如何？）
(A)It's November 1.（今天是十一月一日。）
(B)It's autumn.（現在是秋天。）
(C)It's windy and cold.（有點風也有點冷。）
(D)It's eight o'clock.（現在八點。）
答案：(C)

9. My mum prefers tea to coffee.（我媽媽寧可喝茶不喝咖啡。）
(A)So is my brother.（我弟弟也是。）
(B)Neither is my brother.（我弟弟也不是。）
(C)So does my brother.（我弟弟也是。）
(D)Neither does my brother.（我弟弟也不是。）
答案：(C)

10. What is the typical Japanese food?（典型的日本食物是什麼？）
(A)Hot dogs.（熱狗。） (B)Raisin Scones.（葡萄乾鬆餅。）
(C)Sushi.（壽司。） (D)Rice dumplings.（粽子。）
答案：(C)

11. Shall we hold a food festival to raise some money for the poor students?
（我們為貧困的學生舉辦一場美食展來籌募資金好嗎？）
(A)What a pity!（真可惜。）
(B)That's a great idea.（太棒了。）
(C)What is a food festival?（美食展是什麼？）
(D)We hold it at school.（我們在學校舉辦。）
答案：(B)

12. Can you show me the way to the nearest police station?
（你能告訴我去警察局最近的路線嗎？）
(A)I don't know.（我不知道。）
(B)The police station is over there.（警察局在那裡。）
(C)Walk for two blocks and then turn right.（走過兩個街口之後右轉。）
(D)The police station isn't far.（警察局不遠。）
答案：(C)

Ⅲ、Listen to the dialogue and choose the best answer to the question you hear. （根據你所聽到的對話和問題,選出最恰當的答案。）(6 分)

13. W: When were you born?（W: 你什麼時候生的？）
M: I was born on June 30.（M: 我六月三十日生的。）
W: So you're one month older than I.（W: 這樣你就比我大一個月。）
Q: When was the girl born?（Q: 女孩什麼時候生的？）
(A)On June 13.（六月十三日。）
(B)On July 30.（七月三十日。）
(C)On June 30.（六月三十日。）
(D)On July 13.（七月十三日。）
答案：(B)

14. M: What festival do you like best, Lily?（M: Lily，妳最喜歡哪個節日？）
W: I like the Spring Festival best because I can get some red packets from my parents.（W: 我最喜歡春節，因為爸媽會給我一些紅包。）
M: I like Mid-autumn Festival. I think the mooncakes are the most delicious food in the world.（M: 我喜歡中秋節。我覺得月餅是世界上最好吃的食物。）
Q: What festival does Lily like best?（Q: Lily 最喜歡哪個節日？）
(A)The Spring Festival.（春節。）
(B)Mid-autumn Festival.（中秋節。）
(C)Lantern Festival.（元宵節。）
(D)Dragon Boat Festival.（端午節。）

答案：(A)

15. M: How do you keep in touch with your parents, Mary?
（M: Mary，妳如何跟妳的父母保持聯絡？）
W: I often talk with them on the phone. I call them twice a week.
（W: 我通常跟他們講電話。我一星期給他們打兩次電話。）
M: Why not talk with them on the computer? It's much cheaper.
（M: 為什麼不跟他們在電腦上聊天？那便宜多了。）
Q: How often does Mary call her parents?（Q: Mary 多久給她父母打一次電話？）
(A)Once a day.（一天一次。） (B)Once a week.（一星期一次。）
(C)Twice a day.（一天兩次。） (D)Twice a week.（一星期兩次。）
答案：(D)

16. W: What present have you got for John, Eddie?
（W: Eddie，你要給 John 什麼禮物？）
M: A puppy. John likes dogs very much.（M: 一隻小狗。John 非常喜歡狗。）
W: Don't you know he likes hot dogs better?（W: 你不知道他更喜歡熱狗嗎？）
Q: What can we learn from the dialogue?
（Q: 我們可以從這段對話中知道些什麼？）
(A)John doesn't like hot dogs.（John 不喜歡熱狗。）
(B)John likes hot dogs.（John 喜歡熱狗。）
(C)The girl will give John a puppy.（女孩要給 John 一隻小狗。）
(D)Eddie will give John a hot dog.（Eddie 要給 John 一條熱狗。）
答案：(B)

17. W: How old is your father, Jack?（W: Jack，你父親幾歲？）
M: Oh, I'm fifteen now. My father is thirty-one years older than I.
（M: 喔，我現在十五歲。我父親比我大三十一歲。）
Q: How old is Jack's father?（Q: Jack 的父親幾歲？）
(A)Forty-two.（四十二歲。） (B)Forty-six.（四十六歲。）
(C)Sixty-four.（六十四歲。） (D)Thirty-one.（三十一歲。）
答案：(B)

18. M: Tomorrow is Tree-planting Day. We'll go to plant trees on the beach.
（M: 明天是植樹節。我們要去海灘種樹。）
W: That's great.（W: 太棒了。）
Q: What season is it?（Q: 現在是什麼季節？）

(A)Spring.（春天。）　(B)Summer.（夏天。）
(C)Autumn.（秋天。）　(D)Winter.（冬天。）
答案：(A)

Ⅳ、Listen to the dialogue and decide whether the following statements are True (T) or False (F).（判斷下列句子內容是否符合你所聽到的對話內容,符合的用"T"表示,不符合的用"F"表示。）(6分)

Today is November 26th. It is Thanksgiving Day. The weather is fine. In the evening, Jenny and her mother went to her grandparents' home. When they got there, her cousin Tom was already there. Her grandmother was cooking a big turkey for them. Her grandfather was helping her grandmother in the kitchen. He was making some apple pies. When they saw Jenny, they gave her a big hug and laughed happily. Tom was playing with his toy horse. He was very happy when he saw Jenny. After one hour, they had a delicious dinner together. After the meal, Jenny and her mother went home. What a happy Thanksgiving Day today!

今天是十一月二十六日，感恩節。天氣很好。傍晚 Jenny 和她母親去祖父母家。當她們到了的時候，她的堂弟 Tom 已經在那兒了。她祖母正為他們煮一隻大火雞。她祖父在廚房幫她祖母的忙。他做了一些蘋果派。他們一看到 Jenny，就開心地笑着擁抱她。Tom 在玩他的玩具馬。他看到 Jenny 非常高興。一個小時後，他們一起享用美味的晚餐。用餐過後，Jenny 和她母親就回家了。今天真是一個快樂的感恩節啊！

19. Today is Thanksgiving Day.（今天是感恩節。）
答案：(T 對)

20. Jenny and her father went to her grandparents' home in the evening.
（傍晚 Jenny 和她父親去她祖父母家。）
答案：(F 錯)

21. Jenny's grandmother cooked a turkey for them.
（Jenny 的祖母為他們煮了一隻火雞。）
答案：(T 對)

22. Jenny's grandmother made some apple pies.（Jenny 的祖母做了一些蘋果派。）
答案：(F 錯)

23. Tom was playing with his toy horse when Jenny saw him.

（Jenny 看到 Tom 的時候，Tom 正在玩他的玩具馬。）

答案：(T 對)

24. After the meal, Jenny and her father still stayed there.

（用餐過後，Jenny 和他父親仍然待在那兒。）

答案：(F 錯)

V、Listen and fill in the blanks. (**根據你所聽到的內容,用適當的單詞完成下面的句子。每空格限填一詞。**)(6 分)

Japanese food is getting more and more popular. The most famous is sushi, which you can buy in the supermarkets all around the world. It's expensive to eat in the restaurants. You can save a lot of money by making it yourself. And it's easy. There are lots of different ways of making sushi. Here is one way.

日本食物越來越普遍。最有名的是壽司，你在世界各地的超級市場裡都可以買得到。在餐廳裡吃壽司很貴。自己做的話就可以省很多錢。而且作法很簡單。壽司有很多不同的作法。以下是其中一種做法。

1. Put some sugar, salt and vinegar in a cup.

1. 在杯子裡放一些糖、鹽和醋。

2. Boil some rice in two cups of water to make rice a little harder.

2. 用兩杯水煮米，這樣可以讓飯硬一點。

3. Put the rice into a large bowl. Add half a cup of vinegar.

3. 把飯放進一個大碗裡。加半杯醋。

4. Mix until the rice sticks together.

4. 混合攪拌直到飯黏在一起。

5. Make balls of rice. Each one should be about the size of a table tennis ball.

5. 做飯糰。每一個飯糰的大小差不多和桌球一樣大。

6. Cut the salmon into pieces, then press the salmon on top of the rice balls.

6. 把鮭魚切成片狀，然後把鮭魚壓在飯糰上。

7. Serve the sushi with green tea.

7. 以綠茶搭配著壽司來吃。

25. Japanese food is getting more and more popular.
日本食物越來越普遍。

26. The most famous Japanese food is sushi, which you can buy in the supermarkets all around the world.
最有名的日本食物是壽司，你在世界各地的超級市場裡都買得到它。

27. It's expensive to eat in the restaurants.
在餐廳裡吃壽司很昂貴。

28. You can save a lot of money by making it yourself. And it's easy. There are lots of different ways of making sushi. Here is one way.
自己製作的話就可以省很多錢。作法很簡單。壽司有許多不同的作法。以下是其中一種作法。

29. Put some sugar, salt and vinegar in a cup.
在一個杯子裡放一些糖、鹽和醋。

30. Cut the salmon into pieces, then press the salmon on top of the rice balls.
把鮭魚切成片狀，然後把鮭魚壓在飯糰上。

全新國中會考英語聽力精選(上)原文及參考答案

Unit 8

I 、Listen and choose the right picture.(根據你所聽到的內容，選出相應的圖片。)
(6分)

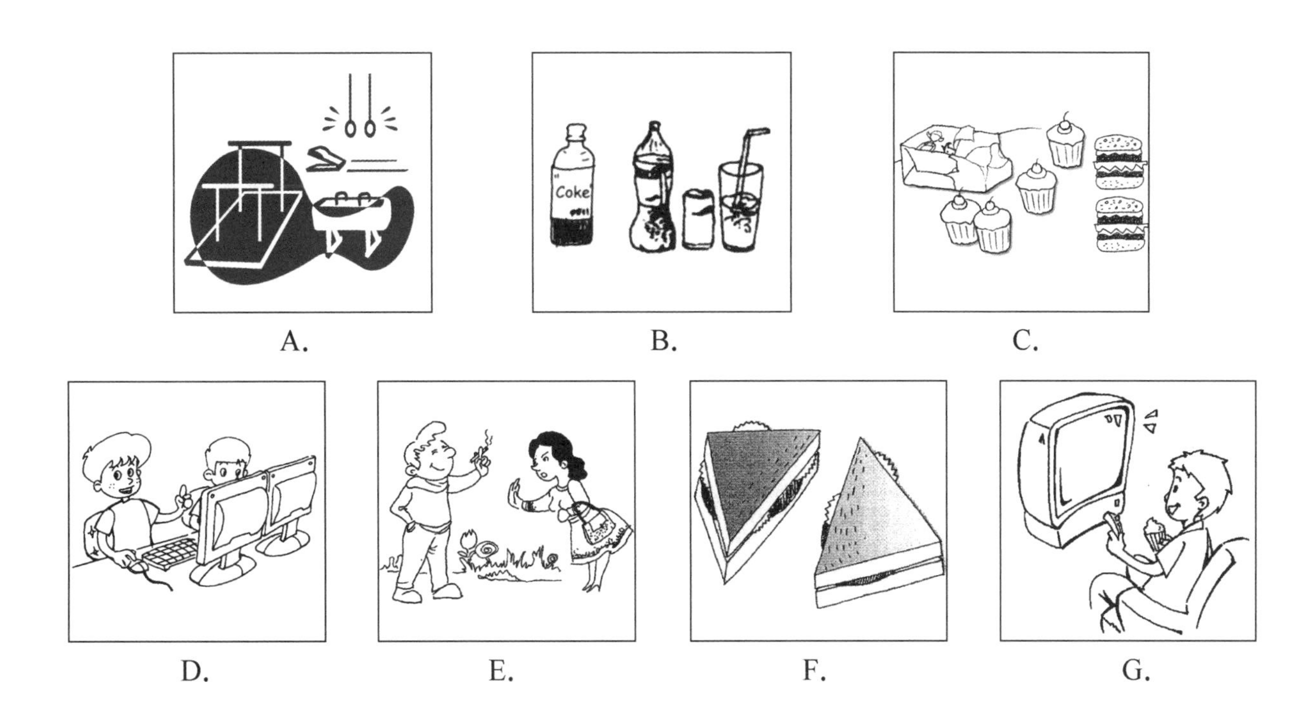

A. B. C. D. E. F. G.

1. Eating too many ice creams or hamburgers will make you quite fat and unhealthy.
(吃太多冰淇淋或漢堡會讓你相當肥胖而且不健康。)
答案：(C)

2. Joe, I think you have played computer games for too long. Your eyes look red and you are always very tired.
(Joe，我想你電腦遊戲玩太久了。你的眼睛看起來很紅而且你老是很累。)
答案：(D)

3. Do you think it is right to sit in the sofa, watching TV and eating ice creams all day long?
(你覺得整天坐在沙發上、看電視、吃冰淇淋是對的嗎？)
答案：(G)

4. Don't drink too much cola or other soft drinks. They may make your bones crispy.
（不要喝太多可樂或其他碳酸飲料。他們可能讓你的骨頭易碎。）
答案：(B)

5. You should give up smoking. It's bad for your health.
（你應該戒菸。那對你的健康不好。）
答案：(E)

6. More and more young people like going to gyms to do some exercise after a whole day's work.
（越來越多年輕人喜歡在一整天的工作之後去健身房運動。）
答案：(A)

Ⅱ、Listen and choose the best response to the sentence you hear.（**根據你所聽到的句子，選出最恰當的應答句。**）（6 分）

7. I like playing badminton very much.
（我非常喜歡打羽毛球。）
(A)So have I.（我也要。）
(B)Neither have I.（我也不要。）
(C)So do I.（我也喜歡。）
(D)Neither do I.（我也不喜歡。）
答案：(C)

8. Shall we go swimming this afternoon?
（我們今天下午去游泳好嗎？）
(A)Thank you very much.（非常感謝你。）
(B)I'm afraid I can't go with you. I have something important to do.
（我怕我不能跟你去。我有些重要的事要做。）
(C)It's very kind of you.
（你真好。）
(D)I'm very sorry to tell you that the water is very dirty.
（我非常抱歉地告訴你，那個水非常髒。）
答案：(B)

9. What should we do to stay healthy?
（我們該做甚麼來保持健康呢？）

(A)We should eat more sweets and fewer vegetables.
（我們應該多吃甜食少吃蔬菜。）

(B)We should exercise regularly.
（我們應該規律地運動。）

(C)We don't need to get up very early.
（我們不需要太早起床。）

(D)We must follow our teacher's advice.
（我們必須遵守老師的忠告。）

答案：(B)

10. What may happen if you eat a lot of sweet food every day?
（如果你每天吃大量甜食可能會發生甚麼事？）

(A)You will need to drink a lot of water.
（你要喝很多水。）

(B)You may get fat.
（你可能變胖。）

(C)You must give up the habit of eating too much sweets.
（你一定要放棄吃太多甜食的習慣。）

(D)You need to go to the gym.
（你需要去健身房。）

答案：(B)

11. My eyes hurt and I have a sore throat.
（我的眼睛很痛，我也喉嚨痛。）

(A)Really?（真的嗎？）

(B)I'm sorry to hear that.（很遺憾聽到那件事。）

(C)Do you feel much better now?（你現在覺得好點嗎？）

(D)Why do you come here?（你為什麼來這裡？）

答案：(B)

12. I watched too much TV and ate too many crisps, I think.
（我想我看太多電視，而且吃太多脆片。）

(A)It doesn't matter much.（那沒甚麼關係。）

(B)Do you know about it?（你知道嗎？）

(C)You should change your bad habits.（你應該改變你的壞習慣。）

(D)It's OK.（那還好。）

答案：(C)

Ⅲ、Listen to the dialogue and choose the best answer to the question you hear.（根據你所聽到的對話和問題，選出最恰當的答案。）(6分)

13. M: Here's the card. How long can I keep the book?
（M: 給你這張卡。這本書我可以保留多久？）

W: Two weeks, sir.
（W: 先生，兩個星期。）

Question: Where are they talking?
（問題：他們在哪裡說話？）

(A)In the school canteen.（在學校餐廳。）

(B)In the library.（在圖書館。）

(C)In a bookshop.（在書店。）

(D)On the playground.（在遊樂場。）

答案：(B)

14. W: What's Alice wearing today?
（W: Alice今天穿甚麼？）

M: She's wearing a red T-shirt, a black skirt, and a pair of white sports shoes.
（M: 她穿一件紅色T恤，一件黑色裙子，和一雙白色運動鞋。）

Question: What color is Alice's skirt?
（問題：Alice的裙子是甚麼顏色？）

(A)Red.（紅色。）

(B)White.（白色。）

(C)Green.（綠色。）

(D)Black.（黑色。）

答案：(D)

15. W: When will you go on a school camping trip?
（W: 你甚麼時候要去學校的露營之旅？）

M: Next week.
（M: 下星期。）

W: Who will go with you?
（W: 誰跟你一起去？）

M: Eight of my classmates.
（M: 我的八個同學。）

Question: How many students will go on a school camping trip?
（問題：有多少學生要去學校的露營之旅？）

(A)Seven.（七個。）

(B)Eight.（八個。）

(C)Nine.（九個。）

(D)Ten.（十個。）

答案：(C)

16. W: May I know your sister's age?
（W: 我可以知道你妹妹的年齡嗎？）

M: She's two years younger than I. I'm twelve.
（M: 她比我小兩歲。我十二歲。）

Question: How old is the boy's sister?
（問題：男孩的妹妹幾歲？）

(A)Ten years old.（十歲。）

(B)Twelve years old.（十二歲。）

(C)Fifteen years old.（十五歲。）

(D)Eight years old.（八歲。）

答案：(A)

17. M: Where's Tom?
（M: Tom 在哪裡？）

W: He has gone to Australia.
（W: 他已經去澳洲了。）

M: Has he been there before?

（M: 他以前去過那裡嗎？）

W: Of course. He was born in Sydney.

（W: 當然。他在雪梨出生。）

Question: Where was Tom born?

（問題：Tom 在哪裡出生？）

(A)In the USA.（在美國。）

(B)In Paris.（在巴黎。）

(C)In New York.（在紐約。）

(D)In Australia.（在澳洲。）

答案：(D)

18. M: May I have some chocolates?

（M: 我能吃點巧克力嗎？）

W: No, you may not. It's time for bed.

（W: 不，你不能吃。現在是睡覺時間。）

Question: Why can't the boy eat any chocolates?

（問題：為什麼男孩不能吃巧克力？）

(A)He has toothache.（他牙痛。）

(B)He has just got up.（他剛起床。）

(C)He doesn't like sweet food.（他不喜歡甜食。）

(D)He has to go to bed.（他必須去睡覺。）

答案：(D)

Ⅳ、Listen to the passage and decide whether the following statements are True (T) or False (F).（判斷下列句子內容是否符合你所聽到的短文內容，符合的用"T" 表示，不符合的用"F" 表示。）(6 分)

The manager of the factory was talking to a young man.

（工廠的經理在對一位年輕人說話。）

The young man wanted to ask for a job.

（那位年輕人想要找一份工作。）

The manager was surprised when the young man said he was asking for high pay.
（當年輕人說他要求高薪的時候，經理很訝異。）

So he asked him, "You don't have much experience. Then doesn't it seem to you that you're asking for too much?"
（所以他問年輕人：「你沒有太多經驗。你難道不覺得你要的太多嗎？」）

"That's right. Since I know nothing about the job, the work for me will certainly be harder than for others. So I should get more money."
（「是的。因為我對這份工作一無所知，所以這份工作對我來說一定比其他的困難。所以我應該得到更多錢。」）

19. The manager was having a talk with a young man.
（經理在跟一位年輕人說話。）
答案：(T 對)

20. The young man and the manager are friends.
（年輕人和經理是朋友。）
答案：(F 錯)

21. The manager was surprised because the young man asked for a lot of money, but he could almost do nothing.
（經理很訝異因為年輕人要求很多錢，但是他幾乎做不了任何事。）
答案：(T 對)

22. The manager thought that the workers in the factory should get the same pay.
（經理認為工廠裡的工作人員應該有相同的薪資。）
答案：(F 錯)

23. The young man said he should be better paid because he would work harder than others.
（年輕人說因為他會比其他人更努力工作，所以他應該有更好的薪水。）
答案：(F 錯)

24. The manager won't employ the young man.
（經理不會雇用那個年輕人。）
答案：(T 對)

V、Listen to the dialogue and complete the table.（根據你所聽到的對話內容，用適當的單詞完成下面的表格。每空格限填一詞。）（6 分）

W: David, you look very healthy. Have you always been so fit?
（W: David，你看起來非常健康。你的身材一直都這麼好嗎？）

M: No. I used to be overweight. I had a very unhealthy diet. I liked junk food like fried chicken and chips.
（M: 不。我曾經過重。我的飲食習慣非常不健康。我喜歡像炸雞、薯條之類的垃圾食物。）

W: How come you've become so fit now?
（W: 你身材現在怎麼變得這麼好？）

M: I took the doctor's advice and went on a diet.
（M: 我聽從醫生的建議節食。）

W: Really? What do you eat now?
（W: 真的嗎？你現在吃些甚麼？）

M: I eat lots of fresh fruit and vegetables, and I eat more fish than meat.
（M: 我吃很多新鮮蔬菜水果，而且我吃魚比吃肉來得多。）

W: What about drinks?
（W: 飲料呢？）

M: I used to be fond of sweet drinks like cola and Sprite, but now I prefer water and fruit juice instead. I also play more sports than before.
（M: 我以前喜歡甜的飲料，像是可樂和雪碧。但是我現在寧可喝水和果汁。我運動也比以前做得多。）

W: No wonder you're so healthy now.
（W: 怪不得你現在好健康。）

	BEFORE（以前）	NOW（現在）
FOOD （食物）	junk food like __25__ chicken and __26__ （垃圾食物，像是____雞和____）	__27__ fruit and vegetables, more __28__ than meat （____水果和蔬菜，____比肉多）
DRINK （飲料）	__29__ drinks （____的飲料）	__30__ and fruit juice （____和果汁）

25. 答案：fried (炸)

26. 答案：chips (洋芋片)

27. 答案：fresh (新鮮的)

28. 答案：fish (魚)

29. 答案：sweet (甜的)

30. 答案：water (水)

全新國中會考英語聽力精選(上)原文及參考答案

Unit 9

I 、Listen and choose the right picture.（根據你所聽到的內容，選出相應的圖片）（5 分）

1. Dogs don't like fish. Give them some bones to chew.
（狗不吃魚。給牠們一些骨頭去咬。）
答案：(E)

2. My parents and I went to the supermarket this morning. We bought a lot of fruit.
（今天早上我和我爸媽一起去超級市場。我們買了很多水果。）
答案：(A)

3. Ben drank up the milk and left home. He didn't eat the bread.
（Ben 喝了牛奶然後出門。他沒吃麵包。）
答案：(C)

4. Kitty, you need to do some exercise. Only eating and no exercising will make you a fat girl.
（Kitty，你需要做些運動。光吃不運動會讓你變成一個胖女孩。）

答案：(F)

5. We usually go to see my grandparents at weekends. We usually have dinner together.
（我們常在周末去看我祖父母。我們常一起吃晚飯。）
答案：(B)

II、Listen and choose the right word you hear in each sentence.（根據你所聽到的句子，選出正確的單字。）(5分)

6. There are a lot of food stalls at the market.（在市場有許多小吃攤。）
(A)snake（蛇）　(B)snail（蝸牛）
(C)stall（攤子）　(D)snack（點心）
答案：(C)

7. Shall we go to Carrefour to buy some food and drink for the coming picnic?
（我們去家樂福為即將來到的野餐買一些食物和飲料好嗎？）
(A)she（她）　(B)short（短的）
(C)shall（將要/…好嗎？）　(D)sheet（一張/一片）
答案：(C)

8. Why not buy some chicken wings? They are very tasty.
（為什麼不買一些雞翅膀呢？它們非常美味可口。）
(A)will（將會/意志）　(B)wing（翅膀）
(C)win（贏得）　(D)wish（希望/祝願）
答案：(B)

9. I don't like peppers because they are too spicy.
（我不喜歡辣椒因為它們太辣了。）
(A)spicy（辣）　(B)speak（說）
(C)sport（運動）　(D)special（特殊的）
答案：(A)

10. Would you like to try some coffee? If you think it's bitter, you can add in some sugar.

（你想要來點咖啡嗎？如果你覺得苦，你可以加點糖。）

(A)better（更好的） (B)bitter（苦的）

(C)bit（一點點） (D)biscuit（餅乾）

答案：(B)

Ⅲ、Listen and choose the best response to the sentence you hear.（根據你所聽到的句子，選出最恰當的應答句。）（5 分）

11. What's the weather like today?（今天天氣如何？）

(A)It's Friday today.（今天是星期五。）

(B)It's 2 May today.（今天是五月二日。）

(C)It's windy today.（今天有風。）

(D)On Saturday afternoon.（在星期六上午。）

答案：(C)

12. May I have some spicy sausages, please?（我想要來點辣香腸，好嗎？）

(A)No, thanks.（不，謝謝。）

(B)OK. Here you are.（好的。給你/在這兒。）

(C)It's all right.（那沒關係。）

(D)That's a good idea.（那是個好主意。）

答案：(B)

13. Shall we buy some bananas?（我們買一些香蕉好嗎？）

(A)OK. That's a good idea.（好。那是個好主意。）

(B)Me too.（我也是。）

(C)Shall we? （我們可以嗎？）

(D)Thank you.（謝謝你。）

答案：(A)

14. Where can we get some prawns?（我們可以在哪裡買到明蝦？）

(A)At the meat section.（在肉品區。）

(B)At the vegetable section.（在蔬菜區。）

(C)At the fruit section.（在水果區。）

(D)At the seafood section.（在海鮮區。）

答案：(D)

15. Would you like some chicken wings, Judy?（Judy，你想要來點雞翅膀嗎？）

(A)Yes. Here we are.（是的，我們到了。）

(B)No, thanks.（不，謝謝。）

(C)That's all right.（沒關係。/不客氣。）

(D)Nice to meet you.（很高興認識你。）

答案：(B)

Ⅳ、Listen to the dialogue and choose the best answer to the question you hear.
（根據你所聽到的對話和問題，選出最恰當的答案。）（5 分）

16. M: May I have some chocolates?（M: 我可以來點巧克力嗎？）

W: No, you may not. It's time for bed.
（W: 不，你不可以。現在是上床睡覺的時間了。）

Question: Why can't the boy eat some chocolates?
（問題：男孩為什麼不能吃巧克力？）

(A)Because he has eaten too much.（因為他吃太多了。）

(B)Because there is none at home.（因為沒有人在家。）

(C)Because it's time to go to bed.（因為是上床睡覺的時間了。）

(D)Because his mother is out.（因為媽媽出去了。）

答案：(C)

17. M: Do you like to watch TV, Jane?（M: Jane，你看電視嗎？）

W: Yes, I do, Tom. But I only watch it at weekends.
（W: 是的，Tom，我看。但是我只在周末的時候看。）

Question: Does Jane watch TV every day?
（問題：Jane 每天看電視嗎？）

(A)Yes, she does.（是的，她每天看。）

(B)No, she doesn't.（不，她不是。）

(C)Yes, he does.（是的，他每天看。）

(D)No, he doesn't.（不，他不是。）

答案：(B)

18. M: Are you going to get up at six tomorrow?
（M: 你明天六點起床嗎？）

W: No, I'm going to get up at seven or eight. You know, it's Saturday tomorrow.
（W: 不，我七點或八點起床。你知道的，明天是星期六。）

Question: What day is today?（問題：今天是星期幾？）

(A)Friday.（星期五。）

(B)Saturday.（星期六。）

(C)Sunday.（星期天。）

(D)Monday.（星期一。）

答案：(A)

19. M: What is John doing now? Is he doing his homework?
（M: John 現在在做甚麼？他在做功課嗎？）

W: No. He is helping his mother with the housework.
（W: 不。他在幫他的媽媽做家事。）

Question: What is John's mother doing?
（問題：John 的媽媽在做甚麼？）

(A)She's doing the housework.（她在做家事。）

(B)She's helping her son with his homework.（她在幫他的兒子寫功課。）

(C)He's doing his homework.（他在寫功課。）

(D)He's helping his mother with the housework.（他在幫他媽媽做家事。）

答案：(A)

20. M: Is there a shop near your school?（M: 你學校附近有商店嗎？）

W: Yes, there is. We can buy things after half past eight in the morning and before a quarter to nine in the evening.
（W: 有。我們可以在早上八點半以後、晚上八點四十五以前買東西。）

Question: What time does the shop close?
（問題：商店甚麼時候關門？）

(A)It open at 9.30 a.m.（它早上九點半開門。）

(B)It closes at 9.15 p.m.（它晚上九點半關門。）

(C)It opens at 8.30 a.m.（它早上八點半開門。）

(D)It closes at 8.45 p.m.（它晚上八點四十五分關門。）

答案：(D)

V、Listen to the passage and decide whether the following statements are True (T) or False (F).（**判斷下列句子內容是否符合你所聽到的短文內容，符合的用 T 表示，不符合的用 F 表示。**）(5 分)

Chinese people like to eat rice with delicious chicken, prawns or beef for dinner.（中國人的晚餐喜歡吃米飯配美味的雞肉、明蝦或牛肉。）

They eat a lot of vegetables, too.（他們也吃很多蔬菜。）

Some people have fruit after dinner.（有些人在晚餐後吃水果。）

Many of them like to drink a lot of tea.（大部分的人喜歡喝很多茶。）

People in Britain often eat beef, spicy sausages and baked potatoes for dinner.（英國人的晚餐通常吃牛肉、辣香腸和烤馬鈴薯。）

They usually have ice cream after meals.（他們通常在餐後吃冰淇淋。）

Some people really like to have a picnic in the garden at weekends.（周末的時候有些人非常喜歡在花園野餐。）

American people like fast food very much.（美國人非常喜歡吃速食。）

The cheapest fast food might be hot dogs.（最便宜的速食可能是熱狗。）

You can see people having hot dogs in the streets or in their cars.（你可以看到人們在街上或他們的車子裡吃熱狗。）

American people also like eating out.（美國人也喜歡出去吃。）

They usually have dinner in the fast food restaurants.（他們通常在速食餐廳吃晚餐。）

21. All Chinese people like to have fruit after dinner.
（所有的中國人喜歡在晚餐後吃水果。）
答案：(F 錯)

22. British people eat a lot of fresh vegetables.
（英國人吃很多新鮮水果。）

答案：(F 錯)

23. British people usually have ice cream after meals.
(英國人常在餐後吃冰淇淋。)
答案：(T 對)

24. British people like to have a picnic in the garden.
(英國人喜歡在花園野餐。)
答案：(T 對)

25. Hamburgers are the cheapest fast food in America.
(漢堡是美國最便宜的速食。)
答案：(F 錯)

Ⅵ、Listen to the passage and complete the notes. (**根據你所聽到的短文內容，用適當的單詞或數字完成下面的筆記。每空格限填一個單字或數字。**) (5 分)

In my family, my father usually does the shopping. (在我家，我爸爸常去購物。)
He always goes shopping at Rose Garden Supermarket.
(他總是在 Rose Garden 超級市場買東西。)
The supermarket is not far away from our home. (超級市場離我家不遠。)
He goes there once a week, usually on Sundays.(他一個禮拜去一次，通常在星期天。)
My mother is good at cooking. (我媽媽喜歡煮飯。)
She cooks for us every day. (她每天為我們煮飯。)
I like the food she cooks. (我喜歡她煮的食物。)
At weekends, she always makes special meals such as spicy sausages and fruit salad. (周末的時候，她總是做好吃的餐點，像是辣香腸和水果沙拉 。)

Shopping (購物)：	Cooking (煮飯)：
Who? __26__ (誰？)	Who? Mother (誰？媽媽)
Where? Rose __27__ Supermarket (在哪兒？玫瑰____超級市場)	What? __29__ sausages (甚麼？____香腸) fruit __30__ (水果____)
When? On __28__ (何時？在____煮飯。)	When? At weekends (何時？在周末。)

26. 答案：Father（父親）

27. 答案：Garden（花園）

28. 答案：Sundays（星期天）

29. 答案：spicy（辛辣的）

30. 答案：salad（沙拉）

全新國中會考英語聽力精選(上)原文及參考答案

Unit 10

Ⅰ、Listen and choose the right picture.（根據你所聽到的內容，選出相應的圖片）（5分）

1. Take the food away. I don't want to eat any food. I'm on a diet.
（把食物拿走。我不想吃任何食物。我在節食。）
答案：(B)

2. Pass me the salt, please, Danny.
（Danny，請把鹽遞給我。）
答案：(C)

3. Mum is shopping at the supermarket now.
（媽現在在超級市場買東西。）
答案：(A)

4. We will go on a picnic this coming Saturday if it is fine.
（如果天氣很好，我們將在下個星期六去野餐。）
答案：(F)

5. Children always like eating sweet food, like ice cream.
（孩子們總是喜歡吃甜食，像是冰淇淋。）

答案：(E)

Ⅱ、Listen and choose the right word you hear in each sentence.（**根據你所聽到的句子，選出正確的單字。**）(5 分)

6. Give me the list. Let me check what you will buy.
（給我清單。讓我檢查你要買甚麼。）

(A)litter（廢棄物） (B)list（清單/列表）
(C)letter（信件） (D)little（少/小）

答案：(B)

7. Shall we buy some fruit like apples and strawberries for the picnic?
（我們去為野餐買些水果，像是蘋果和草莓，好嗎？）

(A)food（食物） (B)foot（腳）
(C)fruit（水果） (D)for（為.../給...）

答案：(C)

8. Wait for the soup to cool.（等湯涼了。）

(A)country（國家/鄉村） (B)cousin（表兄弟姊妹）
(C)cool（冷的） (D)cut（割/切）

答案：(C)

9. What's the matter with you? You are all wet.（你怎麼了？你都濕透了。）

(A)week（週） (B)word（字）
(C)let（讓/使） (D)wet（濕）

答案：(D)

10. On a cold night, a girl went into a forest and never came back.
（在一個冷冷的夜晚，一個女孩走進森林後就再也沒回來了。）

(A)night（夜晚） (B)light（光）
(C)right（正確的） (D)height（高度）

答案：(A)

Ⅲ、Listen and choose the best response to the sentence you hear.（**根據你所聽到的句子，選出最恰當的應答句。**）（5 分）

11. Judy, put the paper in the litter bin.（Judy，把那張紙放進垃圾桶裡。）

(A)Fine, thanks.（好，謝謝。）

(B)Good.（很好。）

(C)All right.（好的。）

(D)No, I can't.（不，我不能。）

答案：(C)

12. Please turn down the TV. I'm doing my homework.

（請將電視音量關小。我在做功課。）

(A)I'm sorry. I'll turn it down.（對不起。我會關小聲。）

(B)What?（甚麼？）

(C)No, I'm watching TV.（不，我在看電視。）

(D)My pleasure.（我的榮幸。）

答案：(A)

13. I'm hungry. Can I have some cakes?（我餓了。我可以吃點蛋糕嗎？）

(A)Yes, it is.（是的，它是。）

(B)No, it isn't.（不，它不是。）

(C)Of course.（當然。）

(D)Yes, you are.（是的，你是。）

答案：(C)

14. How much is the ball?（那個球多少錢？）

(A)It's five.（五點。）

(B)It's over there.（它在這裏。）

(C)It's five yuan.（五元。）

(D)It's your ball.（它是你的球。）

答案：(C)

15. Are there any stamps on your desk?（你桌上有沒有郵票？）

(A)Yes, they are.（是的，它們是。）

(B)Yes, there are.（是的，有。）

(C)No, they aren't.（不，他們不是。）

(D)OK.（好。）

答案：(B)

Ⅳ、Listen to the dialogue and choose the best answer to the question you hear.
（根據你所聽到的對話和問題，選出最恰當的答案。）(5 分)

16. M: Do you usually get up at half past five, Kitty?
（M: Kitty，你通常在五點半起床嗎？）

W: No, my mother usually gets up at half past five. I usually get up at six.
（W: 不，我媽媽通常在五點半起床。我通常在六點起床。）

Question: What time does Kitty's mother get up? (B)
（問題：Kitty 的母親幾點起床。）

(A)5.00 a.m.（早上五點。）

(B)5.30 a.m.（早上五點三十分。）

(C)6.00 a.m.（早上六點。）

(D)6.30 a.m.（早上六點三十分。）

答案：(B)

17. W: Can you speak English, Ben?（W: Ben，你會說英語嗎？）

M: Yes, but just a little. My sister speaks English well.
（M:會，但是只會一點點。我姊姊英語說的很好。）

Question: Who speaks English well?（問題：誰英語說的很好？）

(A)Ben.（Ben。）

(B)Ben's sister.（Ben 的姐姐。）

(C)Ben's brother.（Ben 的哥哥。）

(D)Ben and his sister.（Ben 和他的姊姊。）

答案：(B)

18. W: How many teachers are there in Grade Six?（W: 六年級有多少位老師？）

M: There are fourteen teachers. Eight of them are women teachers.
（M: 有十四位老師。其中有八位是女老師。）

Question: How many men teachers are there in Grade Six?
（問題：六年級有幾位男老師？）

(A)14.（十四。）

(B)8.（八。）

(C)22.（二十二。）

(D)6.（六。）

答案：(D)

19. W: Excuse me, where is the teachers' office?（W: 不好意思，老師辦公室在哪裡？）

M: Sorry, I'm new here, too.（M: 對不起，我也剛來這兒。）

Question: Can the boy help the girl?（問題：那個男孩可以幫助女孩嗎？）

(A)Yes, he can.（是的，他能。）

(B)No, he can't.（不，他沒辦法。）

(C)Yes, he does.（是的，他是。）

(D)No, he doesn't.（不，他不是。）

答案：(B)

20. M: May I play table tennis now?（M: 我現在可以打桌球嗎？）

W: What about your homework today?（W: 你今天的功課呢？）

M: I don't have any homework today.（M: 我今天沒有功課。）

W: Then you may play table tennis.（W: 那麼你可以打桌球。）

Question: What's the boy going to do?（問題：那個男孩要做甚麼呢？）

(A)Play table tennis.（打桌球。）

(B)Do his homework.（做他的功課。）

(C)Help his mother.（幫助他的母親。）

(D)Play tennis.（打網球。）

答案：(A)

V、Listen to the passage and decide whether the following statements are True (T) or False (F).（判斷下列句子內容是否符合你所聽到的短文內容，符合的用 T 表示，不符合的用 F 表示。）(5 分)

Jeff was strong and healthy when he was young.（Jeff 年輕的時候很健康強壯。）

But later he was fat and unhealthy.（但後來他變胖了也不健康。）

He didn't want to get fatter and fatter.（他不想要越來越胖。）

One day, one of his friends said to him, "Would you like to be fit again, Jeff?"
（有一天，有一個朋友跟他說：「你想要再擁有好身材嗎？」）

"Of course!" Jeff answered.（「當然。」Jeff 回答。）

"Well, stop going to your office by car, and go there by bicycle."
（「不要搭車上班，騎腳踏車。」）

Jeff thought this was a good idea.（Jeff 覺得這是一個好主意。）

So he bought a new bicycle from a supermarket and began to go to work by bicycle.
（所以他在超級市場買了一輛新的腳踏車而且開始騎腳踏車上班。）

Jeff thought he would become healthy and strong soon.
（Jeff 覺得他馬上就會變得健康強壯了。）

Riding a bicycle is really a good way for people to keep fit.
（騎腳踏車真的是一個讓人保持身材的好方法。）

21. When Jeff was young, he was fat and unhealthy.
（當 Jeff 年輕的時候，他很胖而且不健康。）
答案：（F 錯）

22. Jeff's friend suggested he go to work by car.（Jeff 的朋友建議他搭車上班。）
答案：（F 錯）

23. Jeff bought a new bicycle from a market.（Jeff 從市場買了一輛腳踏車。）
答案：（F 錯）

24. Jeff would be healthy and strong again because he did some exercise every day.
（Jeff 又變得健康強壯了，因為他每天做運動。）
答案：（T 對）

25. Riding a bicycle can help people keep fit.（騎腳踏車可以幫助人們維持身材。）
答案：（T 對）

Ⅵ、Listen and fill in the blanks.（**根據你所聽到的內容，用適當的單詞完成下面的句子。每空格限填一個單詞。**）（5 分）

M: Excuse me, I am writing a report about people's diet. May I ask you some questions?
（M: 抱歉，我在寫一個關於人們飲食習慣的報告。我可以問你一些問題嗎？）

W: OK. No problem.（W: 好的，沒問題。）

M: Thanks. First, what's your name?（M: 謝謝。首先，你的名字是？）

W: I'm Alice.（W: 我是 Alice。）

M: Well, Alice. How old are you?（M: 好，Alice。你幾歲呢？）

W: I am twenty years old.（W:我二十歲。）

M: Tell me, Alice, what do you usually have for breakfast?
（M: Alice，告訴我，你早餐通常吃甚麼？）

W: I think breakfast is the most important meal of a day. So for breakfast I usually have some milk and some pieces of bread.
（W: 我覺得早餐是一天中最重要的一餐。所以早餐我通常喝牛奶和吃幾片麵包。）

M: Good. What about other meals?（M: 好。其他的餐點呢？）

W: For lunch, I often eat noodles. I also eat a little meat and some fruit salad. For dinner, I usually eat some rice, fish and vegetable soup.
（W: 午餐，我通常吃麵。我也吃一些肉和水果沙拉。至於晚餐，我常吃米飯、魚和蔬菜湯。）

M: Very good! I think you have a healthy diet. Thank you, Alice.
（M: 非常好。我認為你有一套健康的飲食習慣。謝謝你，Alice。）

W: You are welcome.（W: 不客氣。）

- Alice is __26__ years old.
  （Alice ____ 歲。）
- Alice usually has some milk, some pieces of __27__ for breakfast.
  （Alice 的早餐常喝牛奶、吃幾片____。）
- Alice usually has noodles, a little meat and some fruit __28__ for lunch.
  （Alice 的中餐常吃麵條、一些肉，和水果____。）
- Alice usually has some rice, fish and vegetable __29__ for dinner.
  （Alice 的晚餐常吃米飯、魚和蔬菜____。）
- Alice's diet is__30__.

（Alice 的飲食很____。）

26. 答案：twenty/20（二十）
27. 答案：bread（麵包）
28. 答案：salad（沙拉）
29. 答案：soup（湯）
30. 答案：healthy（健康的）

全新國中會考英語聽力精選(上)原文及參考答案

Unit 11

I、Listen and choose the right picture.（**根據你所聽到的內容,選出相應的圖片。**）（6分）

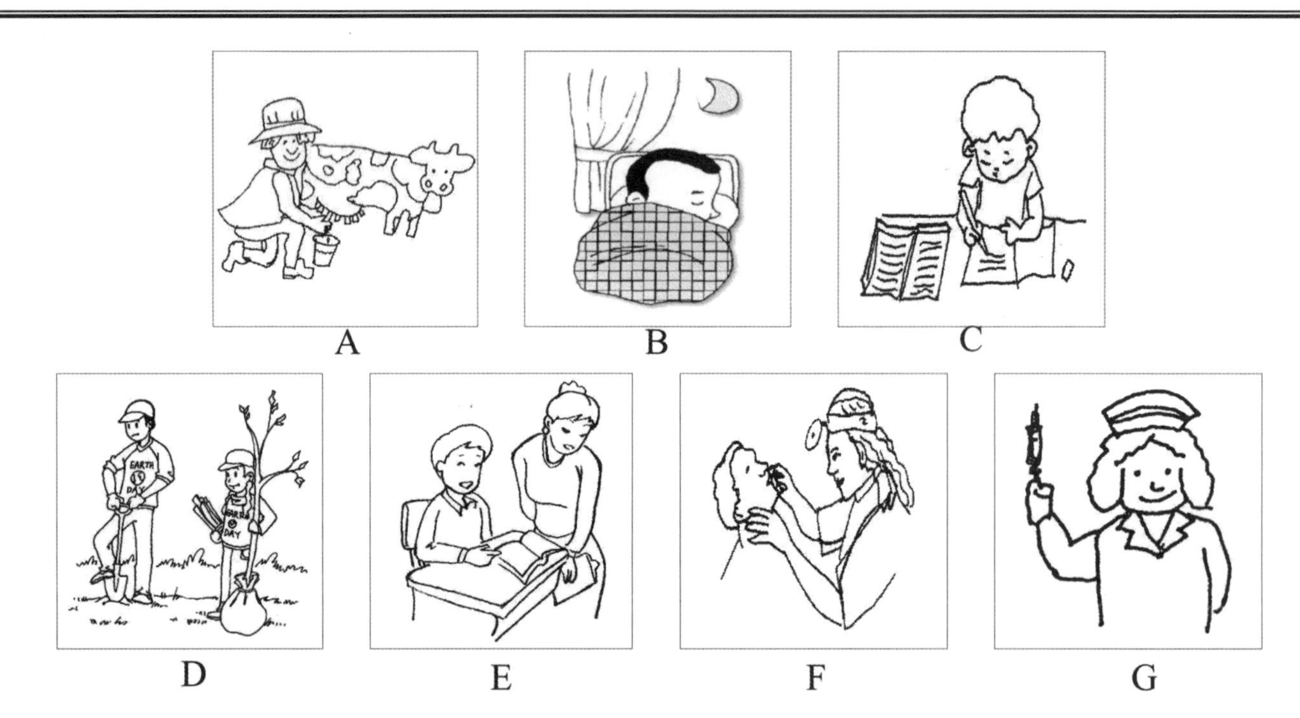

1. The nurse works in No.6 People's Hospital.
（那位護士在第六人民醫院工作。）

答案：(G)

2. The farmer is milking the cow on his farm.
（農夫在他的農場裡擠牛奶。）

答案：(A)

3. Jack sleeps early every evening and he never stays up late.
（Jack 每天晚上很早睡，他從不熬夜。）

答案：(B)

4. Miss Zhang is my Chinese teacher. She is a nice and patient lady.
（Zhang 小姐是我的中文老師。她是一位和藹可親也很有耐心的小姐。）

答案：(E)

5. Yesterday was the Earth Day. Our class planted trees in the park.
（昨天是地球日。我們班在公園種樹。）
答案：(D)

6. John went to the dentist's to have his bad teeth pulled out.
（John 去看牙醫，要把他的壞牙齒給拔掉。）
答案：(F)

II、Listen and choose the best response to the sentence you hear. **(根據你所聽到的句子,選出最恰當的應答句。)(6分)**

7. How often do you go to the library?（你多久去一次圖書館？）
(A)To the library.（去圖書館。） (B)This Sunday.（這個星期天。）
(C)At 3 o'clock.（在三點。） (D)Once a week.（一星期一次。）
答案：(D)

8. The Japanese sushi is very delicious.（日本壽司非常好吃。）
(A)I'm glad you like it.（我很高興你喜歡。）
(B)It's good.（那很好。）
(C)Yes, it is.（是的，它是。）
(D)I'm sorry to hear that.（我很抱歉聽到那件事。）
答案：(A)

9. You'd better eat less sweet food.（你最好少吃甜食。）
(A)That's all right.（沒關係。）
(B)You are welcome.（不客氣。）
(C)Thank you for your advice.（感謝你的忠告。）
(D)No, I won't.（不，我不要。）
答案：(C)

10. What's wrong with you?（你怎麼了？）
(A)I have got a bad cold.（我重感冒。）
(B)I will go to the park tomorrow.（我明天要去公園。）
(C)I am doing my homework.（我在做功課。）
(D)There is something wrong with me.（我有點不大對勁。）
答案：(A)

11. I can't play the guitar.（我不會彈吉他。）

(A)So can I.（我也會）　(B)Neither can I.（我也不會。）

(C)So can't I.（我也不會。）　(D)Neither can't I.（我也不是不會。）

答案：(B)

12. How is your brother?（你的哥哥還好嗎？）

(A)Much better. Thank you.（好多了。謝謝你。）

(B)I'm better. Thanks.（我比較好。謝謝。）

(C)He's writing a report.（他在寫報告。）

(D)You are so kind.（你真好。）

答案：(A)

Ⅲ、Listen to the dialogue and choose the best answer to the question you hear. **（根據你所聽到的對話和問題,選出最恰當的答案。）（6 分）**

13. W: Boys, let's have a 100m running test. Are you ready?

（W: 男孩們，我們來進行一百公尺跑步測驗。準備好了嗎？）

M: Mrs. Wang, my legs were hurt this morning because of a small accident.

（M: Wang 老師，今天早上一場小車禍使我的腿受傷了。）

W: Really? Do you want to go to the clinic?（W: 真的嗎？你要去診所嗎？）

Q: Where does the dialogue probably take place?

（Q: 這段對話大概發生在甚麼地方？）

(A)At the cinema.（在電影院。）

(B)On the school playground.（在學校操場。）

(C)At the clinic.（在診所。）

(D)In the hospital.（在醫院。）

答案：(B)

14. M: What's your plan after you finish school, Betty?

（M: Betty,畢業後妳有甚麼計劃？）

W: Well, my parents want me to be a teacher, but I'd prefer to be a reporter.

（W: 嗯，我父母要我當老師，但是我更喜歡當記者。）

Q: What does Betty want to be after she finishes school?

（Q: 畢業以後 Betty 想當甚麼？）

(A)A teacher.（老師。） (B)A reporter.（記者。）

(C)A doctor.（醫生。） (D)A scientist.（科學家。）

答案：(B)

15. W: What time will the play begin tonight?（W: 今晚表演幾點開始？）

M: It'll begin at eight. When shall we start?

（M: 八點開始。我們該甚麼時後出發呢？）

W: 7 o'clock, OK?（W: 七點好嗎？）

M: The traffic is very heavy at 7. Let's leave half an hour earlier.

（M: 七點交通繁忙。我們提早半小時離開吧。）

Q: When will they leave for the theatre?（Q: 他們幾點前往戲劇院？）

(A)At 6.（六點。） (B)At 7.（七點。）

(C)At 6:30.（六點三十分。） (D)At 7:30.（七點三十分。）

答案：(C)

16. W: I'm so glad it's sunny today. The rain has finally stopped.

（W: 我好高興今天是晴天。雨終於停了。）

M: I hope it will be fine tomorrow, too. We will have a picnic.

（M: 我希望明天天氣也一樣好。我們要去野餐。）

W: But the weather report says it's going to rain again tomorrow.

（W: 但是氣象報告說明天又要下雨了。）

Q: What's the weather going to be like tomorrow?

（Q: 明天的天氣怎麼樣？）

(A)It will be rainy.（會下雨。） (B)It will be cloudy.（會是陰天。）

(C)It will be snowy.（會下雪。） (D)It will be windy.（會有風。）

答案：(A)

17. M: Lily, can you help me with my math?（M: Lily，妳能在數學上幫幫我嗎？）

W: Peter, I would like to. But I'm afraid I am not good at math, either. Tom always gets full marks in math. Let's ask him for help.

（W: Peter, 我很想。但是恐怕我的數學也不怎麼樣。Tom 的數學一直拿滿分。我們去找他幫忙吧。）

Q: Who is good at math?（Q: 誰擅長於數學？）

(A)Lily. (B)Peter. (C)Tom. (D)Jack.

答案：(C)

18. W: Good morning, Dad. What's for breakfast?（W: 爸，早安。早餐吃甚麼？）
M: I've prepared milk, noodles and some bread.
（M: 我準備了牛奶、麵、和一些麵包。）
Q: What hasn't Dad prepared?（Q: 爸爸沒有準備甚麼？）
(A)Milk.（牛奶。） (B)Bread.（麵包。）
(C)Pizza.（披薩。） (D)Noodles.（麵。）
答案：(C)

Ⅳ、Listen to the dialogue and decide whether the following statements are True (T) or False (F).（判斷下列句子內容是否符合你所聽到的對話內容,符合的用"T"表示,不符合的用"F"表示。）（6 分）

Jimmy is a model student at school. He is good at all his subjects except math. But he never gives it up. He always does a lot of math problems. His math teacher also helps him. I think he will be good at math soon. Kitty is a model student, too. She lives far away from school, but she is never late for school. It takes her about 50 minutes to get to school. First, she takes the underground. Then, she takes the bus. Tom is not a model student. He doesn't finish homework on time. In class, he often talks with others. He often fails in exams. Last week, his little brother asked him a very easy question, but he didn't know the answer. Tom felt very sad. He decided to work hard from then on.

Jimmy 在學校是一位模範生。除了數學以外，他所有的科目都很擅長。但是他從不放棄。他一直做很多數學習題。他的數學老師也協助他。我想他的數學很快就會進步。Kitty 也是模範生。她住的離學校很遠，但是她上學從不遲到。她要花五十分鐘去上學。她先搭地鐵。然後再搭公車。Tom 不是模範生。他不準時完成功課。他在班上常常和其他人說話。他考試常常不及格。上個星期，他的弟弟問他一個非常簡單的問題，但是他答不出來。Tom 覺得很難過。從那時候開始他決定努力用功。

19. Jimmy is good at all his subjects.（Jimmy 擅長所有科目。）
答案：(F 錯)

20. Jimmy always does a lot of math problems.（Jimmy 一直做很多數學習題。）
答案：(T 對)

21. It takes Kitty about 40 minutes to get to school.（Kitty 要花四十分鐘去上學。）
答案：(F 錯)

22. Kitty takes a bus first and then she takes the underground.
（Kitty 先搭公車，再搭地鐵。）
答案：(F 錯)

23. Tom couldn't answer his brother's question.（Tom 不能回答他弟弟的問題。）
答案：(T 對)

24. Tom is a model student now.（Tom 現在是模範生。）
答案：(F 錯)

V、Listen and fill in the blanks.（**根據你所聽到的內容,用適當的單詞完成下面的句子。每空格限填一詞。**）(6 分)

Dear Alice,

12 September is my birthday. I'd like to invite you to my birthday party. The party will begin at 6 p.m. at my flat. Many of our friends are coming. We are going to have a barbecue in the garden. We are also going to sing karaoke. We'll watch cartoons, too. I hope you will be free that day. See you then.

Yours,

Jenny

親愛的 Alice，

九月十二日是我的生日。我想邀請你來參加我的生日派對。派對會在我的公寓舉辦，晚上六點開始。我們許多朋友都會來。我們要在花園烤肉。我們也要唱卡拉ＯＫ。我們還要看卡通。我希望你那天有空。到時候見。

你的好朋友

Jenny

全新國中會考英語聽力精選(上)原文及參考答案

Unit 12

I 、Listen and choose the right picture. (根據你所聽到的內容,選出相應的圖片。)(6分)

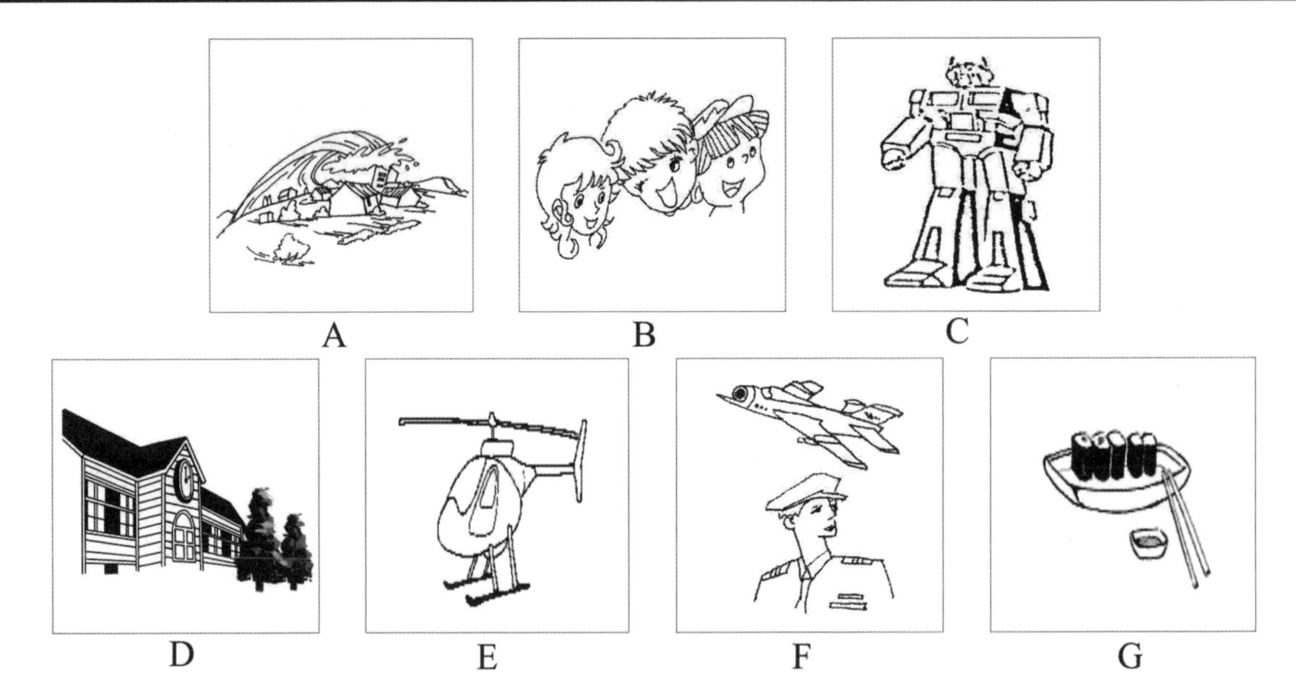

1. The children are discussing what life will be like in the future.
(孩子們在討論未來的生活會是如何。)

答案:(B)

2. Perhaps people will be able to go to work by helicopter in 50 years' time.
(在五十年間內,人們或許可以搭直升機上班。)

答案:(E)

3. I think robots will be very useful in our life in the future.
(我認為機器人在我們未來的生活中將會非常有用。)

答案:(C)

4. My ambition is to be a pilot in the future.
(我未來的志向是要當一名飛機駕駛。)

答案:(F)

5. Sushi is a kind of famous food in Japan.（壽司在日本是一種知名的食物。）
答案：(G)

6. A flood flew away some villages in western part of China last month.
（上個月洪水流經中國西半部的一些村落。）
答案：(A)

II、Listen and choose the best response to the sentence you hear.（根據你所聽到的句子,選出最恰當的應答句。）(6 分)

7. I think perhaps people will be able to live on the Mars.
（我認為人們將有可能住在火星上。）
(A)I think not.（我認為不是。）
(B)I think so, too.（我也這麼認為。）
(C)Yes, I do.（是的，我認為。）
(D)So will we.（我們也會。）
答案：(B)

8. Give me two kilos of tomatoes, please.（請給我兩公斤番茄。）
(A)How much are the tomatoes?（番茄多少錢？）
(B)OK. Ten yuan, please.（好。一共十元。）
(C)The tomatoes are fresh.（番茄很新鮮。）
(D)At the market.（在市場。）
答案：(B)

9. Sorry, I have broken your window, Mr. White.
（White 先生，對不起，我打破你的窗戶了。）
(A)You are welcome.（不客氣。）
(B)Never mind. Take care next time.（別介意。下次小心一點。）
(C)All right.（好的。）
(D)Here you are.（給你。）
答案：(B)

10. What will you say when you invite a friend to a party?
（當你邀請朋友來參加派對的時候你會說甚麼？）
(A)Would you like to come to my party?（你想來我的派對嗎？）

(B)Come to my party.（來我的派對。）
(C)My party is great.（我的派對很棒。）
(D)You must come to my party.（你一定要來我的派對。）
答案：(A)

11. What day is it today?（今天星期幾？）
(A)In the morning.（在早上。） (B)In Japan.（在日本。）
(C)In April.（在四月。） (D)It is Sunday.（今天星期天。）
答案：(D)

12. Can you help me wash the dishes?（你可以幫我洗碗嗎？）
(A)Yes, I can.（是的，我能。） (B)No, I can't.（不，我不能。）
(C)With pleasure.（我很樂意。） (D)Thank you.（謝謝你。）
答案：(C)

Ⅲ、Listen to the dialogue and choose the best answer to the question you hear.（根據你所聽到的對話和問題,選出最恰當的答案。）(6分)

13. W: What kind of film do you like?（W: 你喜歡哪一種電影?）
M: I used to like funny films very much. But now I like action films.
（M: 我以前非常喜歡搞笑片。但是我現在喜歡動作片。）
W: That sounds good! Who is your favourite film star?
（W: 聽起來不錯！誰是你最喜歡的電影明星？）
M: I like Jacky Cheng best.（M: 我最喜歡成龍。）
Q: What kind of film does the boy like now?（Q: 男孩現在喜歡哪一種電影？）
(A)Action films.（動作片。）
(B)Funny films.（搞笑片。）
(C)Documentaries.（紀錄片。）
(D)Love stories.（愛情片。）
答案：(A)

14. W: Excuse me, how much is the red dress?（W: 抱歉，這件紅色洋裝多少錢？）
M: It's 150 yuan.（M: 一百五十元。）
W: What about the white shirt?（W: 這件白色襯衫呢？）
M: 120 yuan.（M: 一百二十元。）
W: OK! I will take both.（W: 好。我兩件都買。）

Q: How much is the woman going to pay?（Q: 這個女人要付多少錢?）

(A)120 yuan.（一百二十元。） (B)150 yuan.（一百五十元。）

(C)270 yuan.（兩百七十元。） (D)300 yuan.（三百元。）

答案：(C)

15. M: It's too far away to go on foot. I think you should take a bus.
（M: 走路去實在太遠了。我認為你該搭公車。）
W: But waiting for buses takes lots of time. I'd like to borrow a bike.
（W: 但是等公車要花好多時間。我想借腳踏車。）
Q: How will the woman go?（Q: 這個女人要怎麼去？）
(A)On foot.（走路。） (B)By bike.（騎腳踏車。）
(C)By bus.（搭公車。） (D)By taxi.（搭計程車。）
答案：(B)

16. M: Where can we go tomorrow, Mary?（M: Mary，我們明天可以去哪兒呢？）
W: We can go to Nanjing Road to do some shopping.
（W: 我們可以去南京路逛街買東西。）
M: You know men hate shopping. What about going to Dongping National Forest Park?（M: 你知道的，男人最討厭購物。去東平國家森林公園怎麼樣？）
W: It's too far. I suggest we go to Shanghai Zoo or Changfeng Park.
（W: 太遠了。我建議我們去上海動物園或是長風公園。）
M: I don't like animals, but I like boating.（M: 我不喜歡動物，但是我喜歡划船。）
Q: Where will they possibly go?（Q: 他們大概會去哪裡？）
(A)Shanghai Zoo.（上海動物園。）
(B)Dongping National Forest Park.（東平國家森林公園。）
(C)Changfeng Park.（長風公園。）
(D)Nanjing Road.（南京路。）
答案：(C)

17. M: What a sunny day, Alice!（M: Alice，今天天氣真好啊！）
W: Yes, it is! Shall we go out for a walk?（W: 對啊！我們去散步好不好？）
M: That's a good idea.（M: 那真是好主意。）
W: Right. I think spring will come soon.（W: 是的。我想春天就快來了。）
Q: What season is it now?（Q: 現在是甚麼季節？）
(A)Spring.（春天。） (B)Summer.（夏天。）
(C)Autumn.（秋天。） (D)Winter.（冬天。）

答案：(D)

18. M: You look so pretty in this green dress with white spots.
（M: 妳穿這件有白色點點的綠色洋裝真好看。）
W: Thank you. In fact, yellow is my favourite, but the shop assistant said there were no yellow dresses at that time.
（W: 謝謝。實際上我最喜歡黃色，但是那時候店員說沒有黃色洋裝了。）
Q: What color is the woman's favourite colour?
（Q: 這個女人最喜歡的顏色是甚麼顏色？）
(A)Green.（綠色。） (B)Yellow.（黃色。）
(C)Blue.（藍色。） (D)Black.（黑色。）
答案：(B)

Ⅳ、Listen to the dialogue and decide whether the following statements are True (T) or False (F).（判斷下列句子內容是否符合你所聽到的對話內容,符合的用"T"表示,不符合的用"F"表示。）（6 分）

In the year 2050, there will be different kinds of materials for clothes. Special chemicals will make the clothes keep clean—they will never get dirty. They will help us save water and money.

到 2050 年，衣物將有不同種類的材質。特殊的化學物質將使衣物保持乾淨——它們永遠不會髒。它們將使我們既省水又省錢。

We won't worry about what to wear to go to school every day. Children won't go to school. They will stay at home in front of their computers. Children can wear their favourite clothes. It will be fun.

我們將不用擔心每天要穿什麼上學了。孩子們將不去學校。他們會待在家裡的電腦前。孩子們可以穿他們最喜歡的衣服。這將會很有趣。

What do you think? Do you think it will be fun? What do you think school clothes and school life will be like in 2050?

你覺得怎麼樣呢？你覺得這樣有趣嗎？到了 2050 年，你覺得校服和學校生活會是怎樣呢？

19. In the year 2015, there will be different kinds of materials for clothes.
（到了 2015 年，衣物將有不同種類的材質。）
答案：(F 錯)

20. The special clothes will easily get dirty.（特殊的衣物將很容易變髒。）

答案：(F 錯)

21. Because of the special clothes, we will save water and money.
（因為有了特殊的衣物，我們將省水又省錢。）

答案：(T 對)

22. Children need to wear uniforms at school every day in 2050.
（到了 2050 年，孩子們每天都要穿制服去學校。）

答案：(F 錯)

23. Children will stay at home and learn things by computer.
（孩子們將在家裡透過電腦來學習。）

答案：(T 對)

24. According to the writer, children will be able to design their favorite clothes.
（根據作者的說法，孩子們將可以設計他們喜歡的衣服。）

答案：(F 錯)

V、Listen and fill in the blanks.（**根據你所聽到的內容,用適當的單詞完成下面的句子。每空格限填一詞。**）(6 分)

M: Why are you looking so disappointed, Tina?

M: Tina，妳怎麼看起來有點失望的樣子？

W: I have just seen the film The Day After Tomorrow. It is a disaster film. The temperature in some parts of the world will keep dropping. And there will be heavy snowstorm and floods everywhere. People will keep shivering.

W: 我剛剛看了「明日過後」這部電影。這是一部災難片。氣溫在世界某些地方會持續下降。到處都有強烈暴風雪和水災。人們一直在發抖。

M: Oh, my God! It's awful. But perhaps things won't be so bad as you think. Although there is terrible air pollution, I think we will be able to solve the problem. For example, plant more trees and drive less cars. Perhaps we can move to another planet by spacecraft. Perhaps we can live in cities under the sea.

M: 天啊！真可怕。但也許事情不是你想的那麼糟。雖然有嚴重的空氣汙染，但我認為我們將有可能解決這個問題。譬如：多種樹，少開車。也許我們可以搭乘太空船移居到另一個星球。也許我們可以住在海底的城市。

W: Maybe you are right, Mike. Let's do something to protect the earth from now on.

W: Mike，你也許是對的。就讓我們從現在開始做些保護地球的事吧。

25. Tina looks disappointed.
Tina 看起來很失望。

26. The temperature in some parts of the world will keep dropping.
氣溫在世界某些地方會持續下降。

27. And there will be heavy snowstorm and floods everywhere.
每個地方都有嚴重的暴風雪和水災。

28. Although there is terrible air pollution, Mike thinks we can solve the problem.
雖然空氣汙染很嚴重，但是 Mike 認為我們可以解決這個問題。

29. Perhaps we can move to another planet by spacecraft.
也許我們可以搭太空船移居到另一個星球。

30. Let's do something to protect the earth from now on.
讓我們從現在起就來做些保護地球的事吧。

全新國中會考英語聽力精選(上)原文及參考答案

Unit 13

I 、Listen and choose the right picture. (**根據你所聽到的內容，選出相應的圖片**)
(5 分)

A. B. C.
D. E. F.

1. When Christmas comes, people in the USA or UK will be busy decorating the Christmas trees.
(耶誕節來臨的時候，美國與英國的人們將忙碌於裝飾耶誕樹。)
答案：(A)

2. You will see a lot of lanterns on the fifteenth day of the first lunar month.
(你將在農曆一月的第十五天看到很多燈籠。)
答案：(F)

3. Woo, such beautiful fireworks!
(哇，多漂亮的煙火。)
答案：(D)

4. Let's go out and enjoy the beautiful full moon tonight.
(讓我們今晚外出欣賞美麗的滿月吧。)

答案：(B)

5. People usually eat rice dumplings to remember Qu Yuan on the Dragon Boat Festival.
（人們通常在端午節吃粽子來紀念屈原。）
答案：(C)

II、Listen and choose the right word you hear in each sentence.（根據你所聽到的句子，選出正確的單字。）（5分）

6. Watching car races is really exciting.（看賽車非常刺激。）
(A)rice（米） (B)race（比賽）
(C)right（對的） (D)rose 玫瑰）
答案：(B)

7. Don't always feel sad. I will always be with you.
（不要總是感到難過。我會一直跟你在一起。）
(A)sad（難過） (B)said（說）
(C)side（旁邊） (D)seed（種子）
答案：(A)

8. Why are you so excited today?（你今天為什麼如此興奮？）
(A)sun（太陽） (B)son（兒子）
(C)some（一些） (D)so（如此）
答案：(D)

9. Qu Yuan was a great poet in Chinese history.
（屈原在中國歷史上是一位偉大的詩人。）
(A)greet（問候） (B)great（偉大的）
(C)grand（雄偉的） (D)read（閱讀）
答案：(B)

10. When do people usually fly kites?（人們通常甚麼時候放風箏？）
(A)kid（小孩） (B)kite（風箏）
(C)cat（貓） (D)kind（種類）

答案：(B)

Ⅲ、Listen and choose the best response to the sentence you hear.（**根據你所聽到的句子，選出最恰當的應答句。**）(5 分)

11. Do you want to go to the flower show?（你想去花卉展覽會嗎？）

(A)Yes, I want.（是的，我想。）

(B)Sorry, I can't.（抱歉，我不能。）

(C)Yes, I do.（是的，我要。）

(D)No, it isn't.（不，它不是。）

答案：(C)

12. Thank you for your help.（謝謝你的協助。）

(A)Welcome, please.（歡迎你，請進。）

(B)All right.（好。）

(C)Yes, please.（是的，請。）

(D)You're welcome.（不客氣。）

答案：(D)

13. What time is it now by your watch?（你的手錶現在是幾點？）

(A)It's Friday.（星期五。）

(B)It's seven.（七點。）

(C)It's fine.（不錯。）

(D)It's 10 October.（十月十日。）

答案：(B)

14. What is he doing now?（他現在在做甚麼？）

(A)He's well. Thank you.（他很好，謝謝你。）

(B)He's doing some shopping.（他正在買些東西。）

(C)He's Mike.（他是 Mike。）

(D)He's a maths teacher.（他是數學老師。）

答案：(B)

15. Can you buy me a ticket?（你可以替我買票嗎？）

(A)Yes, you can.（是的，你可以。）

(B)No, I'm busy.（不，我很忙。）

(C)I'm sorry.（我很抱歉。）

(D)OK.（好。）

答案：(D)

Ⅳ、Listen to the dialogue and choose the best answer to the question you hear.（根據你所聽到的對話和問題，選出最恰當的答案。）(5分)

16. M: What's the date today?（M: 今天幾號？）

W: It's the first of October. It's National Day in China. Mr. Johnson, do you have a National Day in the USA?
（W: 今天是十月一日。是中國的國慶日。Johnson 先生，美國有國慶日嗎？）

M: Yes, we do.（M: 是的，我們有。）

W: When is it?（W: 是哪一天？）

M: It's on the fourth of July.（M: 是七月四日。）

Question: When is National Day in the USA?（問題：美國國慶日是哪一天？）

(A)1 October.（十月一日。）

(B)4 October.（十月四日。）

(C)1 July.（七月一日。）

(D)4 July.（七月四日。）

答案：(D)

17. M: Is Miss Li going to travel to Beijing before New Year's Day?
（M: Li 小姐在新年前要去北京旅行嗎？）

W: Yes, she is.（W: 是的，她是。）

M: Should we buy some presents for her before then?
（M: 我們該在那之前買些禮物給她嗎？）

W: Yes, we could. That's a good idea.（W: 是的，我們應該。那是個好主意。）

Question: When is Miss Li going to travel to Beijing?
（問題：Li 小姐何時去北京旅行？）

(A)On New Year's Day.（在新年。）

(B)On 2 January.（在一月二日。）

(C)Before New Year's Day.（在新年之前。）

(D)In November.（在十一月。）

答案：(C)

18. M: My dad is going to have his birthday tomorrow.
(M:明天是我老爸生日。)
W: What are you going to buy for him?（W: 你要買甚麼給他？）
M: Well, he needs a new watch. So I think I am going to buy him one.
（M: 嗯，我需要一支新手錶。所以我想我會買給他買一支。）
Question: What is the boy going to buy for his father?
（問題：男孩要買甚麼給他父親？）
(A)A tie.（一條領帶。）
(B)A watch.（一支手錶。）
(C)A pair of sunglasses.（一副太陽眼鏡。）
(D)A book.（一本書。）
答案：(B)

19. M: Excuse me, Kate. Would you like to go shopping with me this afternoon?
（M: Kate，不好意思。今天下午你能跟我一起去逛街嗎？）
W: Yes, I'd love to. I like going shopping. Let's meet at the bus stop.
（W: 好，我很樂意。我喜歡逛街。讓我們在公車站碰面。）
M: That's a good place to meet.（M: 那是個碰面的好地方。）
W: See you at about a quarter to three? OK?(W: 大約在兩點四十五分碰面，好嗎？)
Question: What is Kate going to do?（問題：Kate 要去做甚麼？）
(A)To see a film.（看電影。）
(B)To do some shopping.（買東西。）
(C)To visit the museum.（參觀博物館。）
(D)To have dinner with her friend.（和朋友一起吃晚餐。）
答案：(B)

20. M: What's the date today?（M: 今天幾號？）
W: It's the twenty-ninth of September. Oh, it's going to be National Day the day after tomorrow.
（W: 今天九月二十九日。喔，後天就是國慶日了。）
Question: What is the date going to be the day after tomorrow?
（問題：後天將是哪一天？）

(A)29 October.（十月二十九日。）

(B)29 September.（九月二十九日。）

(C)1 October.（十月一日。）

(D)1 November.（十一月一日。）

答案：(C)

V、Listen to the passage and decide whether the following statements are True (T) or False (F).（判斷下列句子內容是否符合你所聽到的短文內容，符合的用 T 表示，不符合的用 F 表示。）(5 分)

The Spring Festival is the Chinese New Year's Day.（春節就是中國新年。）

It usually falls in February.（它通常是在二月。）

Everyone in China enjoys the festival very much.
（每個中國人都非常喜歡這個節慶。）

When the Spring Festival comes, Li Hong usually helps her parents clean the house and do some shopping.
（當春節來臨的時候，Li Hong 通常幫父母清掃房子和買東西。）

On that day everyone in China eats dumplings, New Year's cakes, and other nice food.
（在那一天，每一個中國人吃餃子、年糕和其他好吃的食物。）

Li Hong likes New Year's cakes very much.（Li Hong 非常喜歡年糕。）

But Wang Hai, Li Hong's best friend says dumplings are better than New Year's cakes.
（但是 Wang Hai，Li Hong 最好的朋友，說餃子比年糕好吃。）

Chinese people eat New Year's cakes and dumplings at home.
（中國人在家吃年糕和餃子。）

How happy they are!（他們多開心啊！）

21. The Chinese New Year's Day usually comes in February.
（中國新年通常在二月。）

答案：(T 對)

22. Li Hong usually helps her parents clean the house when the festival comes.
(Li Hong 通常在節日來臨之前幫她父母清掃房子。)
答案:(T 對)

23. Li Hong likes eating dumplings very much.
(Li Hong 非常喜歡吃餃子。)
答案:(F 錯)

24. Wang Hai enjoys eating New Year's cakes very much.
(Wang Hai 非常喜歡吃年糕。)
答案:(F 錯)

25. People always go to restaurants to eat New Year's cakes and dumplings on the festival.
(人們通常在節慶的時候去餐廳吃年糕和餃子。)
答案:(F 錯)

Ⅵ、Listen to the dialogue and complete the table.(根據你所聽到的對話內容,用適當的單詞或數字完成下面的表格。每空格限填一個單詞或數字。)(5 分)

W: I hear you had a nice Open Day. Will you please tell me something about that?
(W: 我聽說你有個很棒的校園開放日。你可以跟我說說嗎?)

M: All right. Last Monday was a sunny day. We had two lessons open to our parents. The first lesson began at five to nine and the second lesson began at ten to ten.
(M: 好。上星期一是晴天。我們有兩堂課開放給我們的父母。第一堂課從八點五十五分開始,第二堂課從九點五十分開始。)

W: Which two classes?(W: 是哪兩堂課?)

M: English and maths.(M: 英語和數學。

W: What was the next?(W: 接下來呢?)

M: Oh, our headmaster gave a report at half past ten.
(M: 喔,我們的校長在十點半提出報告。)

W: When did your parents have lunch?(W: 你們的父母甚麼時候吃午餐?)

M: At twelve.（M: 十二點。）

W: What about afternoon activities?（W: 下午的活動如何？）

M: They began to watch our activities in the English Corner at one and students' performances at a quarter to two. Then at twenty-five to three, the last item, a meeting between our class teachers and parents began.

（M: 他們一點開始在英語角看我們的活動，學生在一點四十五分開始表演。然後在兩點三十五分，最後一個項目，就是父母與我們班導師的會議。）

W: I think all the parents were happy that day.（W: 我想那天所有的父母都很快樂。）

M: Of course.（M: 當然。）

In the morning（早上）	Activities（活動）	In the afternoon（下午）	Activities（活動）
8.55 a.m.（早上8:55）	An English lesson（英語課）	1.00 p.m.（下午1:00）	English Corner（英語角）
9.50 a.m.（早上9:50）	A __26__ lesson（____ 課）	__29__ p.m.（下午____）	Students' performances（學生表演）
__27__ a.m.（早上____）	Headmaster's report（校長報告）	2.35 p.m.（下午2:35）	A __30__ between class teachers and parents（班級導師與家長____）
12.00 a.m.（早上12:00）	__28__（____）		

26. 答案：maths（數學）
27. 答案：10.30（十點三十分）
28. 答案：Lunch（午餐）
29. 答案：1.45（一點四十五分）
30. 答案：meeting（會議）

全新國中會考英語聽力精選(上)原文及參考答案

Unit 14

I、Listen and choose the right picture.（**根據你所聽到的內容，選出相應的圖片。**）（6 分）

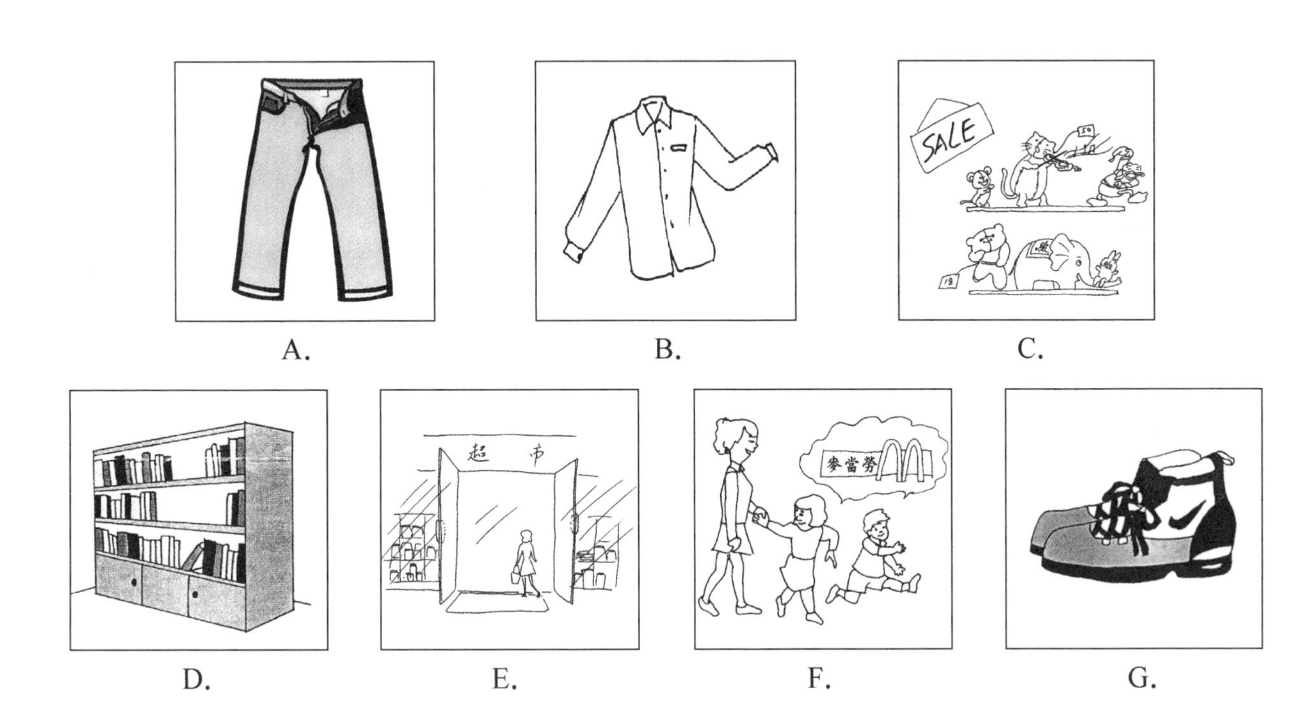

A. B. C. D. E. F. G.

1. Mum, I need a new pair of jeans. The old ones have a hole in them.
（媽，我想要一件新的牛仔褲。舊的這件上面有個洞。）
答案：(A)

2. Oh, Harry, you are old enough. Don't stick in the toy shop every time.
（喔，Harry，你已經夠大了。不要每次都滯留在玩具店。）
答案：(C)

3. Are you hungry, Gary? Let's go to the McDonald's for some food and drinks now.
（Gary, 你餓了嗎？我們現在去麥當勞吃點東西，喝點飲料吧。）
答案：(F)

4. Shall we go to the Sports 100 today? I need to buy a new pair of sports shoes.
（我們今天去 Sports 100 好嗎？我需要買一雙新的運動鞋。）
答案：(G)

5. Linda, we are short of rice, tea and apples. Will you go to the supermarket with me this afternoon?
（Linda，我們的米、茶葉和蘋果都快沒了。你今天下午要跟我去超級市場嗎？）
答案：(E)

6. Look at my study. There aren't enough shelves for me to keep all my new books. Let's go to the furniture shop now.
（看看我的書房。書架已經不夠讓我擺我所有的新書。我們現在去家具店吧。）
答案：(D)

Ⅱ、Listen and choose the best response to the sentence you hear.（**根據你所聽到的句子，選出最恰當的應答句。**）（6分）

7. May I have a look at your new shoes?
（我可以看看你的新鞋嗎？）
(A)Certainly. Here you are.（當然可以。在這裡。）
(B)No, you mustn't.（不，你絕對不可。）
(C)Not at all.（一點也不。）
(D)Yes, I will.（是的，我要看。）
答案：(A)

8. What a sweet voice you've got!
（你的聲音真甜美啊！）
(A)I'm glad you like it.（我很高興你喜歡它。）
(B)Thank you.（謝謝你。）
(C)Please don't say so.（別那麼說。）
(D)Of course not.（當然沒有。）
答案：(B)

9. I'm sorry for giving you so much trouble.
（我很抱歉我帶給你這麼多麻煩。）
(A)All right.（好的。）
(B)Of course not.（當然沒有。）
(C)Never mind.（別介意。）

(D)My pleasure.（我的榮幸。）

答案：(C)

10. Our school team lost the game last night.
（昨天晚上我們的校隊輸了那場球賽。）

(A)Sorry to hear that.（很抱歉聽到那件事。）

(B)Please give them three cheers.（請給他們三次喝采。）

(C)Nothing wrong.（沒有錯。）

(D)It's hard to say.（那很難說。）

答案：(A)

11. What's your English teacher like?
（你的英文老師長得怎麼樣？）

(A)She likes music.（她喜歡音樂。）

(B)She's tall and beautiful.（她很高很漂亮。）

(C)She is well.（她很好。）

(D)She likes me.（她喜歡我。）

答案：(B)

12. What about going for a walk?
（去散步怎麼樣？）

(A)That's all right.（那沒關係。）

(B)So do I.（我也是。）

(C)Why not? Let's.（為什麼不？我們走吧。）

(D)Walking is good to you.（步行對你很好。）

答案：(C)

Ⅲ、Listen to the dialogue and choose the best answer to the question you hear. **（根據你所聽到的對話和問題，選出最恰當的答案。）(6 分)**

13. W: Good morning, Tom. Where are you going?
（W: Tom，早安。你要去哪裡？）

M: Morning, Mary. Going to the language laboratory. And you?
（M: Mary，早安。我要去語言教室。你呢？）

W: To the computer room. I'm going to have a computer lesson.
（W: 去電腦教室。我有一堂電腦課。）

Question: Where is Tom going?
（問題：Tom 要去那裡？）

(A)To the playground.（去遊樂場。）

(B)To the garden.（去公園。）

(C)To the computer room.（去電腦教室。）

(D)To the language laboratory.（去語言教室。）

答案：(D)

14. M: Is your home on the second floor, May?
（M: May，你家在二樓嗎？）

W: Yes, Tom.
（W: Tom，是的。）

M: Oh, my home is two floors higher than yours.
（M: 喔，我家比你家高兩層樓。）

Question: Which floor does Tom live on?
（問題：Tom 住在幾樓？）

(A)On the 1st floor.（一樓。）

(B)On the 2nd floor.（二樓。）

(C)On the 4th floor.（四樓。）

(D)On the 12th floor.（十二樓。）

答案：(C)

15. W: How do you go to your factory every day, John?
（W: John，你每天怎麼去你的工廠？）

M: By bus.
（M: 搭公車。）

W: Is it very far away from here?
（W: 離這裡非常遠嗎？）

M: Yes, it is. Do you go to your office by bus, Mary?
（M: 是的。Mary，你搭公車去你的辦公室嗎？）

W: No, I don't.

（W: 不，我不是。）

Question: Who goes to work by bus?

（問題：誰搭公車去上班？）

(A)John and Mary.（John 和 Mary。）

(B)Mary.（Mary。）

(C)May.（May。）

(D)John.（John。）

答案：(D)

16. M: Which goes more quickly, a bus or a car?

（M: 公車和汽車哪一個比較快？）

W: A car. But a train goes more quickly than a car.

（W: 汽車。但是火車比汽車更快。）

M: You're right.

Question: Which goes most quickly?

（問題：哪一個最快？）

(A)A bike.（腳踏車。）

(B)A train.（火車。）

(C)A car.（汽車。）

(D)A bus.（公車。）

答案：(B)

17. M: Do you get up at a quarter past six, Mary?

（M: Mary，你六點十五分起床嗎？）

W: No, but Jack does. I get up fifteen minutes earlier than he.

（W: 不，但 Jack 是。我比他早十五分鐘起床。）

Question: What time does Mary get up?

（問題：Mary 幾點起床？）

(A)At a quarter past six.（六點十五分。）

(B)At six o'clock.（六點。）

(C)At a quarter to six.（五點四十五分。）

(D)At half past six.（六點半。）

答案：(B)

18. M: Hi, Miss Wang. You came to work on foot today, didn't you?
(M: 嗨，王小姐。你今天走路來上班，對嗎？)

W: Yes, I did.
(W: 是的，我是。)

M: You usually come to work by bike.
(M: 你平時騎腳踏車來上班。)

W: That's right. But my bike is broken now.
(W: 對。但是我的腳踏車壞了。)

Question: How does Miss Wang usually come to work?
(問題：Wang 小姐通常怎麼來上班？)

(A)On foot.（走路。）

(B)By bike.（騎腳踏車。）

(C)By bus.（搭公車。）

(D)By underground.（搭地鐵。）

答案：(B)

Ⅳ、Listen to the passage and decide whether the following statements are True (T) or False (F).（判斷下列句子內容是否符合你所聽到的短文內容，符合的用"T" 表示，不符合的用"F" 表示。）(6分)

George is a young man.
（George 是個年輕人。）

He does not have a wife, but he has a very big dog, and he has a very small car too.
（他沒有妻子，但是有一隻非常大的狗，還有一輛非常小的車。）

He likes playing tennis.
（他喜歡打網球。）

Last Monday he played tennis for an hour at his club, and then he ran out and jumped into a car.
（上星期一他在他的俱樂部打了一小時的網球，然後他跑出去跳上一輛車。）

His dog came after him, but it did not jump into the same car.
（他的狗跟著他，卻沒有跳上同一輛車。）

It jumped into the next one.
（牠跳進另一輛車。）

"Come here, silly dog!" George shouted at it but the dog stayed in the other car.
（「到這裡來，小笨狗！」Geroge 對著狗大叫，但是狗待在另一輛車。）

George put his key into the lock of the car, but the key did not turn.
（George 把他的鑰匙插進車子的鎖，但是鑰匙轉不動。）

Then he looked at the car again.
（所以他再看了看那輛車。）

It was not his!（那不是他的！）

He was in the wrong car!（他進錯了車！）

And the dog was in the right one!（狗在對的車哩！）

"He's sitting and laughing at me!" George said angrily.
（「牠正坐著笑我呢！」Geroge 生氣地說。）

But then he smiled and got into his car.
（但是他後來笑著走進他的車。）

19. George has a wife and a dog.
（Geroge 有一位妻子和一隻狗。）
答案：(F 錯)

20. His car is quite small.
（他的車相當小。）
答案：(T 對)

21. He belongs to a football club.
（他隸屬於一個足球俱樂部。）
答案：(F 錯)

22. After his tennis last Monday, his dog did not get into the car with him.
（上星期一打完網球之後，他的狗沒跟著他進那輛車。）
答案：(T 對)

23. George shouted, and the dog came to him.
(Geroge 大叫，狗走向他。)
答案：(F 錯)

24. The dog was in the right car, and George was in the wrong one.
(狗在對的車裡，George 在錯的車裡。)
答案：(T 對)

V、Listen and fill in the blanks.(**根據你所聽到的內容，用適當的單詞完成下面的句子。每空格限填一詞。**)(6 分)

An important businessman went to see his doctor because he couldn't sleep at night.
(一個重要的商人去看醫生，因為他晚上睡不著。)

The doctor examined him carefully and then said to him, "You need to learn to relax. Have you got any hobbies?"
(醫生仔細的幫他檢查，然後對他說：「你需要學習放鬆。你有任何嗜好嗎？」)

The businessman thought for a while and said, "No, I don't have any time for hobbies."
(商人想了一會兒說：「沒有，我沒時間從事嗜好。」)

"Well," the doctor answers, "that is your main trouble. You don't have time for anything except your work. You must find some hobbies, or you'll die in less than five years. Why don't you learn to paint pictures?"
(「嗯，」醫生回答，「那就是你主要的問題。除了工作以外，你沒時間做其他事。你一定要找出一些嗜好，要不然你不到五年就死了。你何不學著畫圖呢？」)

The next day he phoned the doctor and said, "That was a very good idea. I've already painted fifteen pictures since I saw you."
(隔天，他打電話給醫生說：「那是個好主意。自從我去看你之後，我畫了十五張圖。」)

- An important businessman went to see his doctor because he couldn't __25__ at night.
  (一個重要的商人去看醫生，因為他晚上不能____。)

- The doctor examined him __26__ and asked him if he had any hobbies.
  （醫生____為他檢查，並且問他是否有任何嗜好。）
- The businessman __27__ for a while and told the doctor that he didn't have time for hobbies.
  （商人____了一會兒，對醫生說他沒時間從事嗜好。）
- The doctor told him that he didn't have time for anything __28__ his work and he would die in less than __29__ years if he didn't have any hobbies.
  （醫生告訴他，他____他的工作以外沒時間做其他事。如果他沒有任何嗜好，不到____年他就死了。）
- The businessman told the doctor the next day that he had __30__ painted fifteen pictures since he saw the doctor.
  （商人隔天告訴醫生，自從他看了醫生之後他____畫了十五張圖。）

25. 答案：sleep (睡覺)
26. 答案：carefully (仔細地)
27. 答案：thought (認為/想)
28. 答案：except (除了...之外)
29. 答案：five/5
30. 答案：already (已經)

全新國中會考英語聽力精選(上)原文及參考答案

Unit 15

I、Listen and choose the right picture.(根據你所聽到的內容，選出相應的圖片。)(6分)

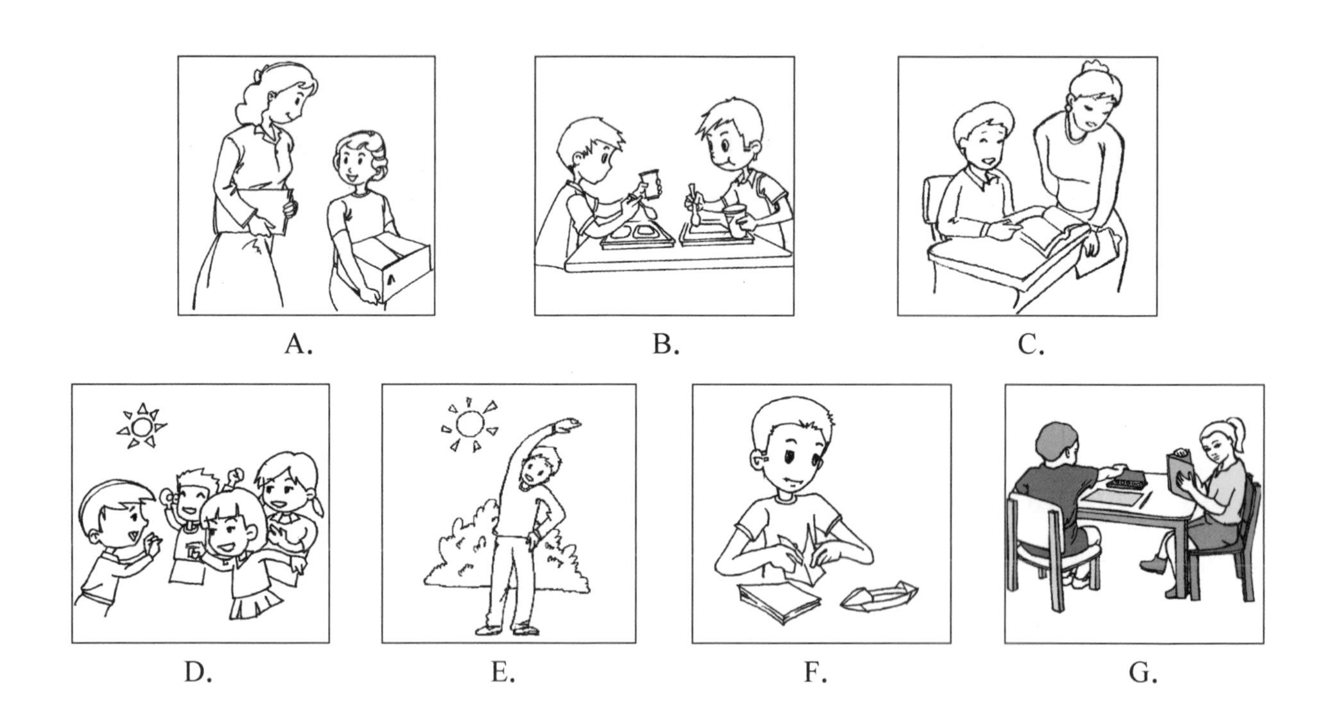

1. Joe is busy with his studies but he does exercise regularly every day.
   (Joe 忙於他的功課，但是他每天規律地運動。)
   答案：(E)

2. Students in middle schools of Shanghai have lunch at school.
   (上海的中學學生在學校吃午餐。)
   答案：(B)

3. Kelly and her classmates always play games after class. Look, they are happy.
   (Kelly 和她的同學總是在課後玩遊戲。看，她們很開心。)
   答案：(D)

4. Alice is a nice girl and now she is helping her English teacher carry something.
   (Alice 是一個好女孩，她現在正在幫她的英文老師拿東西。)
   答案：(A)

5. Susan often helps her brother with his studies.
（Susan 常協助他弟弟的學業。）
答案：(C)

6. It took John a long time to learn how to make paper boats.
（John 花了很長的時間學習如何做紙船。）
答案：(F)

II、Listen and choose the best response to the sentence you hear.（根據你所聽到的句子，選出最恰當的應答句。）(6 分)

7. Where are you going this coming Sunday?
（這個星期天你要去哪裡？）
(A)To the park.（去公園。）
(B)At the library.（去圖書館。）
(C)On foot.（步行。）
(D)With my friend.（跟我朋友一起。）
答案：(A)

8. Kate likes playing tennis.
（Kate 喜歡打網球。）
(A)Let's go.（我們去吧！）
(B)So do I.（我也喜歡。）
(C)Neither do I.（我也不喜歡。）
(D)Yes, I'd love to.（是的，我要打。）
答案：(B)

9. The TV play is wonderful.
（電視劇很棒。）
(A)I like watching TV plays.（我喜歡看電視劇。）
(B)The TV play is on Channel 5.（那個電視劇是在五號頻道。）
(C)We usually watch TV plays at weekends.（我們通常在周末看電視。）
(D)I think so, too.（我也這麼認為。）
答案：(D)

10. Is your sister getting better?
（你姊姊好一點了嗎？）
(A)It's very kind of you.（你真好。）
(B)Yes, much better. Thank you.（是的，好多了。謝謝你。）
(C)She works better than before.（她做的比以前好。）
(D)Yes, I am very well. Thank you.（是的，我很好。謝謝你。）
答案：(B)

11. I think you should do morning exercises every day.
（我覺得你應該每天做早晨運動。）
(A)That's all right.（沒關係。）
(B)Of course.（當然。）
(C)OK. I'll take your advice.（好。我會採納你的意見。）
(D)Never mind.（別介意。）
答案：(C)

12. Miss Lin, I'd like to invite you to the dancing party next week.
（Lin 小姐，我想邀請你參加下星期的舞會。）
(A)I'm busy.（我很忙。）
(B)Yes, please.（是的，請。）
(C)Have a great date.（祝你有個很棒的約會。）
(D)Thank you. I'll be glad to come.（謝謝你。我很樂意前往。）
答案：(D)

Ⅲ、Listen to the dialogue and choose the best answer to the question you hear.
（根據你所聽到的對話和問題，選出最恰當的答案。）(6 分)

13. W: Have you finished all the six maths problems?
（W:六個數學問題你全做完了嗎？）
M: Er, I have finished all of them except No. 6.
（M:哦，除了第六題以外我全都做完了。）
Question: How many problems has he finished?
（問題：他完成了多少個問題？）

(A)Six.（六個。）

(B)Five.（五個。）

(C)Only one.（只有一個。）

(D)Seven.（七個。）

答案：(B)

14. W: Was Jim born in 1978?

（W: Jim 是 1978 年出生的嗎？）

M: Yes, he and Jack are of the same age, two years older than Sam.

（M: 是的，他和 Jack 相同年齡，比 Sam 大兩歲。）

Question: When was Sam born?

（問題：Sam 何時出生？）

(A)In 1979.（1979 年。）

(B)In 1978.（1978 年。）

(C)In 1980.（1980 年。）

(D)In 1977.（1977 年。）

答案：(C)

15. M: Oh, look! These tomatoes are red and big. Would you buy some of them, Madam?

（M: 喔，看看！這些番茄又紅又大。女士，你要買一些嗎？）

W: Yes, I want two kilograms.

（W: 好，我要兩公斤。）

Question: Where are they?

（問題：他們在哪裡？）

(A)In a market.（在市場。）

(B)In a building.（在一棟建築物。）

(C)In a library.（在圖書館。）

(D)In a park.（在公園。）

答案：(A)

16. W: Hello! You look tired today.

（W: 哈囉！我今天看起來很累。）

M: Yes. I went to bed too late last night.
（M: 是的。我昨晚太晚睡了。）

W: You'd better go to bed earlier tonight.
（W: 你今晚最好早點睡。）

Question: Why does the man look tired today?
（問題：那個男人今天為什麼看起來很累。）

(A)Because he didn't go to bed.（因為他沒睡覺。）

(B)Because he went to bed too late last night.（因為他昨晚太晚睡。）

(C)Because he went to bed early last night.（因為他昨晚很早睡。）

(D)Because he slept very well.（因為他睡得很好。）

答案：(B)

17. W: This book costs 12 dollars. I haven't got enough money. Can I borrow 6 dollars from you, Jack?
（W: 這本書價值十二元。我的錢不夠。Jack，我可以跟你借六元嗎？）

M: Sorry. I have only 3 dollars.
（M: 抱歉。我只有三元。）

Question: How much will the woman have if Jack lends her his money?
（問題：如果 Jack 把錢借給那個女人，女人會有多少錢？）

(A)7 dollars.（七元。）

(B)8 dollars.（八元。）

(C)9 dollars.（九元。）

(D)12 dollars.（十二元。）

答案：(C)

18. W: Excuse me, Mr. Smith. Do you come from France?
（W: 不好意思，Smith 先生。你來自法國嗎？）

M: No, I come from America. What about you, Mrs. Brown?
（M: 不，我來自美國。Brown 太太，你呢？）

W: I come from England.
（W: 我來自英國。）

Question: Where does Mr. Smith come from?
（問題：Smith，抱歉先生來自何處？）

(A)France.（法國。）

(B)America.（美國。）

(C)England.（英國。）

(D)Australia.（澳洲。）

答案：(B)

Ⅳ、Listen to the passage and decide whether the following statements are True (T) or False (F).（判斷下列句子內容是否符合你所聽到的短文內容，符合的用"T" 表示，不符合的用"F" 表示。）(6分)

When Kate was eighteen years of age, her mother gave her a beautiful ring.
（當Kate十八歲的時候，她的母親給了她一個漂亮的戒指。）

It was a birthday present and Kate was very pleased.
（那是一個生日禮物，Kate非常開心。）

A week later when she was working in the kitchen, she lost the ring.
（一個星期以後，當她在廚房做事的時候，她掉了那個戒指。）

She looked everywhere in the kitchen but still could not find it.
（她在廚房裡到處找但就是找不到。）

She also looked outside the kitchen but still the ring was not found.
（她也到廚房外面找，但是戒指仍然找不到。）

Kate became very sad.
（Kate非常難過。）

She even cried.
（她甚至哭了。）

In the evening at dinner time, her brother, Peter, was eating some cakes.
（傍晚吃晚餐的時候，她的哥哥Peter在吃蛋糕。）

"They are very good cakes! Who made them?"
（「這些蛋糕非常好！誰做的？」）

"I made them," Kate said.
（「我做的。」Kate說。）

She was glad that her brother liked the cakes she made.
（她很高興她哥哥喜歡她做的蛋糕。）

She was very fond of cooking.
（她非常喜歡烹飪。）

“Are there any more? Oh!” he started to ask, “Mum, this is a strange kind of cake.”
（「還有嗎？噢！」他發問，「媽，這是一種奇怪的蛋糕。」）

Kate was excited.
（Kate 很訝異。）

“My ring!” she cried.
（「我的戒指！」她大叫著。）

She took it to the kitchen, washed it and then came back.
（她把戒指拿去廚房，洗乾淨之後又回來。）

She thanked her brother.
（她感謝她的哥哥。）

“I'm sorry you got such a surprise,” she said, “but thank you very much for finding my ring. I'll cook some more nice cakes for you tomorrow.”
（「很抱歉你遇到這樣的驚喜。」她說，「但是非常感謝你找到我的戒指。我明天會做更多蛋糕給你。」）

19. Kate got a ring as her eighteenth birthday present.
（Kate 有一個戒指是她的十八歲生日禮物。）
答案：(T 對)

20. Kate lost the ring outside the kitchen.
（Kate 在廚房外面掉了那個戒指。）
答案：(F 錯)

21. Kate was good at making cakes.
（Kate 擅長做蛋糕。）
答案：(T 對)

22. Kate's brother found the ring in one of the cakes she had made.
（Kate 的哥哥在她做的某一個蛋糕裡找到那個戒指。）
答案：(T 對)

23. Kate didn't like the ring very much.
（Kate 不是很喜歡那個戒指。）

答案：(F 錯)

24. Kate decided to make her brother some more cakes for finding the ring.
(因為找到了戒指，所以 Kate 決定為他哥哥做更多蛋糕。)
答案：(T 對)

V、Listen and fill in the blanks. (**根據你所聽到的內容，用適當的單詞完成下面的句子。每空格限填一詞。**)(6 分)

Television has now come to nearly every family.
(電視現在幾乎進入了每個家庭。)

It has become a very important part in people's life.
(它在人們的生活中變得非常重要。)

School children in the USA watch TV about twenty-five hours a week.
(美國的學童一個星期大約看二十五個小時的電視。)

Soon people feel that television is good for children because it helps them learn about their country and the world.
(很快的，人們發現電視對兒童有益，因為電視幫助他們認識他們的國家與世界。)

With the help of programs of education, children do better in school.
(在教育節目的協助下，兒童在學校表現得更好。)

Other people feel that there are too many programs about love and crime on TV, and that even programs of education don't help children a lot.
(其他人認為電視上有太多關於愛情與暴力的節目，甚至教育性節目對孩子來說幫助並不大。)

Children simply watch too much television, so they don't do a lot of other important things for their education.
(因為兒童看太多電視，所以他們在教育學習上做不了更多其他重要的事。)

Children of three to six learn to speak their language and talk with people.
(三到六歲的兒童要學習語言、與他人說話。)

When they are watching TV, they are only listening to the language, and they aren't talking with anyone.
(當他們看電視的時候，他們只能聽語言而不與任何人說話。)

When school children watch TV, they read less.
（當學童看電視的時候，他們較少閱讀。）

Because of this, they don't learn to read or write quickly at school.
（因為如此，他們在學校無法快速學習閱讀與寫字。）

All children learn by doing, and they need time to play in order to learn about the world.
（所有的兒童從做中學習，他們需要時間遊戲來認識這個世界。）

When they watch TV, they play less.
（當他們看了電視，他們玩得少。）

They also have less time to spend with their parents and friends, and they have less time to have sports.
（他們花較少的時間與父母朋友在一起，而且他們運動的時間不多。）

Recently, fifteen families in Denver decided to stop watching TV for a month or more.
（最近，Denver 市的十五個家庭決定一個多月不看電視。）

At first it was difficult, but there were soon a lot of good changes.
（一開始很難，但是他們很快的有了很多很好的改變。）

The children read, played, and exercised more and the family became full of joy.
（兒童閱讀、遊玩、運動的比較多，而且家庭變得充滿樂趣。）

But at the end of the month all the families began to watch TV as much as before.
（但是在那個月結束之後，所有的家庭開始看和以前一樣多的電視。）

Not one family was able to give up television completely.
（沒有一個家庭可以完全放棄電視。）

1. With the help of programmes of education, children do __25__ in school.
（有了教育節目的幫助，兒童在學校表現得____。）

2. Children simply watch too much television, so they don't do a lot of other __26__ things for their education.
（兒童就是看太多電視，所已他們在教育學習上坐不了更多其他____的事。）

3. When children are watching TV, they are only __27__ to the language, and aren't talking with anyone.
（當兒童看電視的時候，她們只能____語言，而不與任何人說話。）

4. When school children watch TV, they read __28__.
（當學童看電視的時候，她們較____閱讀。）

5. All children learn by doing, and they need time to play in order to learn about the __29__.
（所有的兒童從做中學，而且她們需要時間遊戲來認識這個____。）

6. At first, stopping watching TV for a month was difficult, but there were soon a lot of good __30__.
（一開始，一個月不看電視很難，但是很快的就有了很多很好的____。）

25. 答案：better (較好的)

26. 答案：important (重要的)

27. 答案：listening (聆聽)

28. 答案：less (較少的)

29. 答案：world (世界)

30. 答案：changes (改變/變化)

全新國中會考英語聽力精選【上】

出版者：夏朵文理補習班
出版發行：禾耘圖書文化有限公司
地址：新北市新店區安祥路109巷15號
電話：02-29422385　傳真：02-29426087
劃撥帳號：50231111禾耘圖書文化有限公司

總經銷：紅螞蟻圖書有限公司
地址：台北市114內湖區舊宗路2段121巷28號4樓
網站：www.e-redant.com
電話：02-27953656　傳真：02-27954100
劃撥帳號：16046211紅螞蟻圖書有限公司
ISBN：ISBN 978-986-94976-0-2　(上冊：平裝)

出版日期:106年6月

本書由華東師範大學出版社有限公司授權
夏朵文理補習班出版發行

定價420元